THE TEENAGE WORRIER'S
POCKET COLLECTION

www.kidsatrandomhouse.co.uk

THE TEENAGE WORRIER'S POCKET COLLECTION

Ros Asquith

CORGI BOOKS

THE TEENAGE WORRIER'S POCKET COLLECTION
A CORGI BOOK 0 552 548391

Published in Great Britain by Corgi Books,
an imprint of Random House Children's Books

Corgi edition first published as a WHS exclusive edition in 2001
This edition published in 2003

1 3 5 7 9 10 8 6 4 2

Collection copyright © Ros Asquith, 2001

including:
THE TEENAGE WORRIER'S POCKET GUIDE TO ROMANCE
First published in Great Britain by Corgi Books, 1998
Copyright © Ros Asquith, 1998

THE TEENAGE WORRIER'S POCKET GUIDE TO FAMILIES
First published in Great Britain by Corgi Books, 1998
Copyright © Ros Asquith, 1998

THE TEENAGE WORRIER'S POCKET GUIDE TO MIND & BODY
First published in Great Britain by Corgi Books, 1998
Copyright © Ros Asquith, 1998

THE TEENAGE WORRIER'S POCKET GUIDE TO SUCCESS
First published in Great Britain by Corgi Books, 1998
Copyright © Ros Asquith, 1998

The right of Ros Asquith to be identified as the author of this work has been
asserted in accordance with the Copyright, Designs and Patents Act 1988.

Papers used by Random House Children's Books are natural, recyclable products made
from wood grown in sustainable forests. The manufacturing processes
conform to the environmental regulations of the country of origin.

Set in 11½ pt Linotype Garamond by
Phoenix Typesetting, Ilkley, West Yorkshire.

Corgi Books are published by Random House Children's Books,
61–63 Uxbridge Road, London W5 5SA,
a division of The Random House Group Ltd,
in Australia by Random House Australia (Pty) Ltd,
20 Alfred Street, Milsons Point, Sydney, NSW 2061, Australia,
in New Zealand by Random House New Zealand Ltd,
18 Poland Road, Glenfield, Auckland 10, New Zealand,
and in South Africa by Random House (Pty) Ltd,
Endulini, 5A Jubilee Road, Parktown 2193, South Africa

THE RANDOM HOUSE GROUP Limited Reg. No. 954009
www.kidsatrandomhouse.co.uk

A CIP catalogue record for this book is available from the British Library.

Printed and bound in Great Britain by
Cox & Wyman Ltd, Reading, Berkshire.

THE TEENAGE WORRIER'S POCKET GUIDE TO ROMANCE

Ros Asquith

as Letty Chubb

CORGI BOOKS

CONTENTS

we have so much in common

Heart-shaped pillow
Waterbed
Luxury Suite
ROMANTIC Wayside Inn
Lurvers' Lane
Remotesville
Isle of View
Hotsex
KISS
1LUV U2

Dearest Teenage Worrier(s),

Is there a certain someone who makes your heart race like drum'n'bass, your legs feel bendier than silly string, your face feel as if each cheek had turned into a grilled tomato? Do you weep deep into the night? Gaze for hours at a time at blurry photo? Keep fragments of lurved one's old chewing-gum under tear-stained duvet?

Here, at long last, is the handy Pocket Guide that brings you all the secrets of True ROMANCE: how to find the perfect partner; how to trap them in a willy (sorry, wily) NET; how to KEEP them there by stunning ruses such as, um, knowing how to stimulate their vital **zones** (phew, hurl self into ice bucket) and how to be V.V.V. Interesting while remaining elusively Kooool Etck.

I shall also be showing how to avoid all those tragic ROMANTIC worries that plague the life of the average spotty, greasy, pudding or beanpole-shaped Teenage

Worrier of the twenty-first century.

Such as: MUST I really go out with someone when I am V. Happy by myself? HAS everyone else on planet had sex except moi? WHEN that V.V. Attractive, dazzling, witty, intelligent person ignores me as though I were a mere ant, does it really mean they lurve me but are too kool to show it? OR is it they just don't care for the name 'Ant', arf arf, argh Etck. (NB Quick answers to the above questions are no, no and um (sorry), no.

It will tell you all about **Dates**: How to get one; How to avoid one; How to look; What to do . . . How Not to Care too much. How to say get lost, get found Etck.

As my fan(s) will know, I haven't quite solved all of these myriad lurve-worries moiself just yet, but in the process of writing this advice-packed tome, I am sure I will advance to greater self-knowledge and enhance my ability to entrap any passing male that takes my fancy. I feel V.V. Highly qualified to talk of such matters now, as I have actually KISSED three whole boyz (well, akshully, only bits of their faces of course, ahem). I think this is a V. High number for someone of my humble age (although if you listened to some of the liars at my skule you wd think they had Done It with everyone in Universe) although I must admit that in each case I have only kissed them once, so I that I have still not, um, Gone the Whole Way, nor am I likely to until I am well over the age of consent, due to:

1) Lack of opportunity
2) Fear of breaking law

2

3) Fear of catching terminal illness
4) Fear of not knowing what bit to put where (will this buke help?)
5) Lack of interest (not mine, the boyz; they are always looking over my shoulder at my frend Hazel)

ROMANCE, anyway, is different to sex. It is about longing, dreaming, hoping, wanting, yearning, swooning, lusting, slavering, snogging (whoops, phew, ice bucket again).

So put away that box of tissues, close your ears to the screech of violins and the wail of banshees that make the life of a Teenage-Worrier-in-Lurve so tragic and learn how to, um, think positive (wish I could) and look on Bright Side (bright side of what?). In short, I will expose all the daft advice other bukes land you with and hope that by the time you've got from A to Z, you will either get happy in ROMANCE or throw this buke at the moron who doesn't care about you.

And go on to better boyz. Or gurlz.

—Lurve, as ever,

Letty Chubb

X X

An INTRO TO MOI . . .

A few werds about the ROMANCES of my life so
far, full details of which you can find soulfully
relayed in my three previous tomes . . .

Brian 'Brain' Bolt

Not exactly right for ROMANCE category, as
although Brian faithfully cleaves to *moi*, I would
really prefer to spend the day with my little
brother's gerbil, Horace, who, come to think of it
rather resembles Brian but lives much more exciting
life. If a three-metre-high Valentine card arrives on
Feb *13th* in order to embarrass the householder and
give the recipient a day in which to return the
favour, it will have Brian's exquisite copperplate
hand upon it. But it is not his spots, or his fluffy
teeth, that put me off Brian. It is more his obsessive,
doggy devotion to *moi*. And, of course, that incident
with the bicycle wheel and the flour . . .

Daniel Hope

The first true lurve of my LIFE, Daniel Hope still
has hair the colour of wet sand at sunset (I tried to
make *moi*self think it was more the colour of elastic
bands when he left me but – sob – I just couldn't

convince *moi*self) and eyes bluer than forget-me-nots.
Nonetheless he has successfully forgotten-me-often
and has raised my hopes only to cruelly dash them
on the rocks of despair by abandoning me on *three*
separate occasions, twice with two of my best
friends. Tragickly, ROMANCE being what it is, I
know that if I glimpse his manly form, or hear his
sonorous tones, I am liable to swoon. On principle
then, I only allow myself to pass his house (which
involves, I admit, an elaborate detour from my
school route) about four times a week. There is still
something about being on the street where he
lives . . .

Adam Stone

Daniel may be beautiful, but he has a wilful and
negligent soul. Adam, whose hair is like little
bunches of grapes, whose eyes are twin coals
gleaming with mischief and smouldering with
unleashed pashione, is as honest as the Day is Long.
As noble as a knight of olde. As truthful as little
Georgie Washington. And in Los Angeles. It is my
tragedy that he escaped there because I was too
foolish to believe his lurve for *moi* . . . Nightly I
weep into my pillow (I wonder if I shld change
pillowcases more often? Maybe this is why I sneeze
so much) and beat my little fists against the walls in
an agony of tribulation. Did he get my letter
explaining All? Should I write again? I write

5

nightly, but tear up my efforts. Oh, Adammmmmm, Adaaaaaam, is your soul like your surname? Will you never return?

With heavy pen, dear reader, I return to the task of this brief guide, hoping to inject a little hope, a little joy, into my life which is otherwise blighted by failed ROMANCE. Thank goodness I am comforted still by my only faithful lurve – my cat **Rover**. She may make me sneeze even more than my sodden pillow, but at least she is here . . .

NB If you buy loads of this book, maybe I can scrape up the fare to L.A. and see my darling Adam again, even if it is only once . . . even if it is to see him in the arms of Sharon Groan . . .

Adonis

Glorious Youth beloved of Venus, the goddess of Lurve, and therefore a term used to describe V. Fanciable blokes up to the present day. ie: that is, Daniel and Adam (swoon). However, it is V. worth bearing in mind that Brian Bolt may one day be seen as an Adonis by someone or something, possibly a relative of Benjy's gerbil. That day can't come too fast for me. The Adonis is also a pleasant species of butterfly — let no-one accuse me of failing to educate you, dear reader(s).

Attraction

Is that magnetic force that impels you towards someone, drawn by mysterious X-Files-type force Etck. It is as mysterious — and invisible — as the elemental force of gravity on all of earth's inhabitants as discovered by Isaac Newton shortly before going into coma when apple fell on head. The great thing about attraction is, everyone has got some of it. It is not about simple things like having big bazoomz Etck, but about mysterious chemical substances like pheromones, which we all give off and which some people give off more of than others. This partly explains universal oddities like: why is person who looks like the back of a car ferry always pursued by fifty panting hunks? Or hunking pants. Why is V. Beautiful person sad and lonely? Etck.

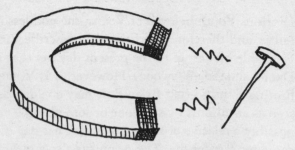

Magnets attract – but also repel. Ask yourself: do you really <u>WANT</u> that nail? No rude remarks about screws, <u>per-LEASE</u>).

However, not being attractive to the person you have set your heart on does not mean you have no pheromones, just that the right person for your particular brand hasn't turned up yet. Also, whether you attract people has as much to do with your own mood as how you look. And this in turn has to do with confidence. Confidence is what we Teenage Worriers need in bucketfuls but usually have only in tiny droplets . . .

But . . . dear fellow Worriers, remember that a ROMANTIC relationship cannot thrive on affection alone, nor must it ever try to survive on pity. It must contain ye elements of *sizzle*. So, however much you LIKE someone, don't bother if you don't fancy them too. It will only lead to heartache (theirs). If it's clear they don't fancy YOU, it will also only lead to heartache (yours). If you fancy them but don't much like them, also steer clear. This could lead to even bigger heartache (cue sound effects of squalling infants, tragick Teenage Worriers alone in endless docs' waiting-rooms Etck).

If only it were so easy...

BACHELORS

Unmarried males. These are what unmarried females are supposed to sniff out and lure into matrimonial web of cozy nest, nuclear family, Happy-Ever-After Etck. 'Nuclear' has always seemed to me a good word to apply to Family Life, due to loud bangs, flying objects, deadly fall-out Etck, but I think it's supposed to mean going round in circles, which is what life in *La Maison Chubb* feels like most of the time.

Beau

My dictionary says 'Fop, dandy, ladies' man', but maybe I shld get a more recent dictionary. Personally I like the term 'Beau', and think that reintroducing it wld enhance quality of ROMANCE. It seems to say yr LURVED one is all the things you want them to be, beautiful inside and out Etck, something to be proud of, and beautiful enough to be proud of you too Etck. That's enough on Beaux, phew, thunder of massed violins Etck.

Bezonian

The opposite. This means 'Rascal, beggarly fellow'. I also hope this isn't a description of Daniel. Wince. 'Ragamuffin' was a pretty old and confusing word to Teenage Worriers and that came back as a streetword, so why not Bezonian? 'Hey, y'all F***in' bezonians in here, shuh man!' That sort of thing . .

HEY, WOW, he's BEZONIAN INNIT?

BLIND DATES

Blind dates are obviously a great idea if you don't
know how to meet someone any other way, and I
imagine as long as you take V. good precautions, ie:
don't give address to stranger Etck, meet in V.
pubic (sorry, public) place and be sure to go home
early on yr own Etck, that they might provide you
with a few moments of fun.

There are several different ways of getting a Blind Date:

1) A dating agency where you pay through nose to feed yr details into a computer and get a 'perfect match' i.e: You say you are a size 25 when breathing in, with a low IQ and no prospects and they magically find you a heartbreakingly handsome, solvent companion looking for just such a one as you. El Chubb is unconvinced, but I have heard of one or two successes in groups of V. old people over 25.

2) Advertise. This enables you to weed out some (but not all) weirdos and usually gives you a chance to check out their appearances. If they do not include photo – hopefully, of their face – ask yourself: why? This method is also more common for old on-shelf (joke) group.

3) Best idea for Teenage Worriers is to get a frend of a frend to fix you up with someone they think you'll like.

As long as you are V. Careful (murderers, sadists Etck have been known to seek their victims through small ads), I think these methods wld be fun. After all, everyone is lonely some of the time and most of us are lonely most of the time, so there is NO SHAME.

Boyz

Must find MY BOY Fancy dress

The fashionable idea that Boyz are aliens from another werld (or, if you are a boy, that gurlz are aliens from another planet) was first introduced to this country by *moi*, in my best-selling buke (puff, plug) *I Was a Teenage Worrier* (still available – my Mother has six copies). However, as I pointed out then and as I still believe, boyz are more like gurlz than:

a) they like to admit
b) gurlz like to admit
c) anything else around

If you don't believe (c) above, then ask yourself, if you are a gurl, the following question: am I more like a boy than say, an armadillo, or an elephant, or a piano stool?

If you are a boy, you may like to wonder: what is more like me? A gurl? Or a cardboard box?

Of course, having established the similarities, we must remind ourselves of the differences.

More gurlz (but not all) paint their nails pale green. More gurlz (but not all) wear V. silly flimsy leg covers that get torn by minute particles of grit so they have to buy another pair after ONE DAY.

More gurlz wear V. short skirts and shave their legs. Etck.

13

Boyz do silly things too. But one of the silliest things boyz do, in the opinion of many (though not all) gurlz, is to pay more attention to round things like footballs and wheels than to round things like us (or straight thingz with V. microscopic round bits like *moi*). In other werds, gurlz do all the nail-painting Etck to attract boys when all boyz really want to do is skulk around in sheds comparing their valve-gear.

True Equality of Ye Sexes can only come when they do stuff which pleases themselves in equal amounts. So, boyz shld get sillier about their appearances (why should a boy in make-up be assumed to be gay?) and gurlz shld get sillier about hobbies, sez L. Chubb. However, for those of you who are interested in dating boyz, here are a handful of types to watch out for:

1) Hamlet
V. Indecisive prince who lurved his Father more than his gurlfriend and ended up killing his gurlfriend's poor old innocent father instead of his wicked uncle cos he couldn't make his mind up what to do. The poor old bloke he killed said 'To Thine own self be True' (note for illiterate Worriers: this means Be True to Yourself) which seems V. Good advice to me and more useful on ROMANCE's merry-go-round than Hamlet's 'To Be or Not to Be'. Gnash, Worry.

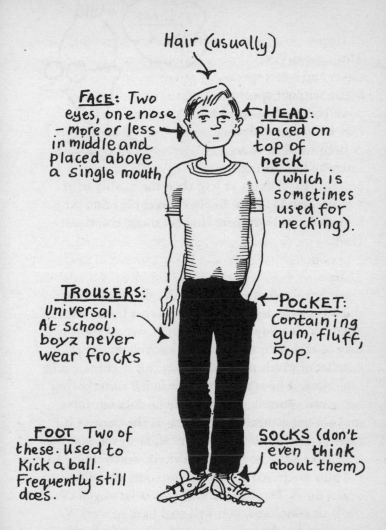

Hair (usually)

FACE: Two eyes, one nose - more or less in middle and placed above a single mouth

HEAD: placed on top of neck (which is sometimes used for necking).

TROUSERS: Universal. At school, boyz never wear frocks

POCKET: Containing gum, fluff, 50p.

FOOT Two of these. Used to kick a ball. Frequently still does.

SOCKS (don't even think about them)

Points of a <u>BOY</u> – illustrating L. Chubb's thesis that BOYZ are more like GIRLZ than anything else on Planet Earth... (so end sexist krap now) sez Chubb.

2) *Boffin*

This type is V.V.V.V.
clevel and wears specs. A
boffin without specs is
not a boffin, although he
may be V. interllekshual.
A Boffin will be more
interested in the quality

of light that falls on yr wig than the quality of yr
wig itself and is more likely to have his mind on
higher things than mare (I mean mere) emotions.
Huh.

3) *Shy*

Gurlz are V. often attracted to V. shy boyz as they
think they are deep. This is often true but is also
often not. If a boy seems too shy to ask you out, it
may be that he is too bored to ask you out, or the
number of words necessary to do it is higher than he
can count. If he is too shy to declare his everlasting
lurve, ask yourself: is it possible he does not lurve
me? Do not assume that shyness is the cause of his
extreme lack of interest in you. If, however, you
really like a shy boy, it is definitely worth trying to
get him interested by asking him out, say half-a-
dozen times. I would think this is as far as you can
go. If this succeeds, you will still have to work V.
hard to get a shy boy interested in you. Since no-one
has ever shown any interest in them before, they will
take a long time to believe you.

4) Sexist Pig

This is a sub-category of Yob, and though Yob behaviour almost always involves Sexist Piggery ('You've 'ad the rest, now try the best, darlin' Etck), some Sexist Pigs are cunningly disguised as non-Yobs and seem V. Interesting and Nice until you realize they expect you to always be at their beck and call, wear what they want, shut up when they're talking Etck.

Avoid this type.

5) Perfecto

This is the one who Has it All and Can Do It All. No point in trying to compete. Basic adulation and flattery usually work, cos the one thing they tend not to be strong on is modesty. But how can you gain their interest? Try to find one thing they're NOT good at (Needlework? Canoeing? Making model cathedrals out of matchsticks?) and devote yourself to it. This will avoid the risk of comparison in other fields and they will hopefully be convinced that you are a committed Eccentric dedicated to Yr Art.

6) Self-Obsessed

They say: 'We've talked enough about me, let's talk about *you* . . . What do you think of my new haircut?'

They ask for one ticket at the box office, even though you paid last time. They walk down Lurvers' Lane running their fingers tenderly through their own hair.

Avoid this type.

7) Insecuresville

'Oh I could never do that' they say admiringly of your teeniest accomplishments, and you are V. charmed. But they really mean it. And they are V.

Sad that they cld never do it. And they go on about how V. Sad they are that they couldn't do it. And on and on and on. V. Exhausting. If you adore an Insecuresville, your patience may be rewarded by their other sterling qualities, although personally I wld prefer to find these without the insecurities (being a V. Insecure sort of person *moi*self, worry, moan, self-doubt, despondency).

8) Beardo
(Male, usually. If a gurl with a beard, you can get it removed by electrolysis, ask yr doc.)

Some Gurlz find beards, moustaches Etck V. Romantic and arty-looking teachers with beards, or V. Caring-looking ones with beards are often the Objects of Crushes. Big bushy beards are popular with Iron John types who thrash around in forests beating their chests, howling, crying, thinking about their Mothers and trying to find their True Selves. If they find them and then have a shave they are V. Welcome to look me up, but I do not fancy kissing a bird's nest. I know it's V. Unfair that men have to shave every day, and that I have a Campaign For Hairy Armpits, Legs Etck, but personal preference only goes as far, in my case, as a soft fuzz of Designer Stubble, though even this can look V. Posey, espesh with leather coat-collar turned up. Anyway, you get the picture. All of you in LURVE with hairy Boyz can relax because they're safe from *moi*.

9) Romeo

One who everyone fancies, but who has eyes only for yoooou. Exists, possibly, but only in your dreams.

(handwritten note:) to Have censored this pic as each of us has own idea of Romeo (sigh).

Breaking Up

There is an old song that says that breaking up is hard to do, and what it means is that it is hard to be left, which we all know, even if it hasn't happened to us yet. But it also means that it is hard to leave someone. Heed the advice of El Chubb: it is much better to be cruel to be kind and tell the truth *now*, rather than in two, three, or worse still thirty years' time. Never stay with someone out of pity, it just won't work. If they are trying to leave you, you have to let them do it too, instead of following first impulse, which is to plait yrself around their speeding limbs and emit long piercing howl. You definitely do not want to have six kids before he makes for the Exit, do not pass Go, do not collect gloom of spouse Etck.

TIPS FOR BREAKING UP

a) Be clear.

b) Be Kind.

c) Do not tell the person you are leaving that they are a bundle of old rubbidge. They will be feeling like that anyway.

d) Do not get back together under any circumstances for AT LEAST a year, even if you ARE lonely and tempted.

e) Remember, you broke up, so there was a REASON for it.

Hard as this is to do, always remember it is much, much worse for the person you are giving the old heave-ho to.

I often feel V. Guilty about my rejection of Brian, particularly since I inflamed his hopes Etck by going out with him again even after I'd told him it wouldn't work sharing gerbil stories with him Etck. This second episode made him miserable and, if it hadn't happened, I'd also still have a perfectly good bicycle . . .

If you are the one who is left, the best thing you can do is feel V.V.V.V. Sorry for yourself for a week. Cry constantly (preferably at a high, keening pitch), play lots of sad music and lock yourself in yr room Etck to Worry yr Mother (or other suitable caring adult) as much as possible, thereby ensuring maximum sympathy and making yourself V. Important to those around you. Over the next three weeks, emerge now and then with doleful expression to take light refreshment and allow yrself to be persuaded to sit in front of telly covered in blankets and weeping.

After one month, pick up relatively normal life. Tell yrself that Person-of-Yr-Dreams was, although perfect, Not Right For You. You cld never be happy with someone who didn't Love-you-as-you-loved-them. There is a worthier person (also better looking, funnier Etck) out there who you have yet to find. Life is worth living without a partner anyway and you are a special worthy person in yr own right Etck Etck.

Say these things to mirror every night. You will be surprised to find that within a few months you will be able to hear your lurved one's name without feeling as if you are going to die. Recovery has begun. It can only get better.

CHATTING UP

Er, sadly, the stumbling attempts of most Teen Worriers at Chatting Up will include the following touching, if naff, exchanges:

YOU: So where did you learn to do that?
HIM: What?
YOU: Hypnotize people with the back of your head. I just gazed at the back of your head for a second

and now I am hopelessly hypnotized and can think of nothing but you and will do whatever you say . . .

(NB Note bad mistake in this approach as it lays you open to total rejection. ie: he says, 'Get lost' and you have to.)

A better approach wld be:

YOU: So where did you learn to do that?
HIM: What?
YOU: Hypnotize people with the back of your head. I just gazed at the back of your head and now I feel that unless I can gaze at the front of it for the rest of my LIFE I will never be completely happy again. May I gaze at it for at least a few more minutes before you cast me into Oblivion?

(This wld take a V. hard-hearted person to refuse.)

I know it wld be V. Nice to be the recipient of such attempts to please, but you cld wait for eternity before a bloke wld summon up the courage to try these out on you, so it is better to practise yourself and not whinge if you are rejected.

CINEMA

Cinema tip: when Person-of-Yr-Dreams invites you to come to *Large Door*, do not take it at face value or as a rude remark about your size, as it will probably be the French movie *L'age D'Or* (Golden Age, to you illiterate monolingualists). This happened to me with Adam and I have since wondered whether I successfully disguised my mistake, or whether he realized at that moment that I was a true Moron.

Tip 2: do not assume that a PG, a 12 or even a U are for babies. The cinema classifications are so daft that a little bit of swearing (much less than you hear in the average household before breakfast) will shoot a film from U to 15 in milli-seconds, whereas violence quite unsuitable for one of my little brother Benjy's tender age will happily be classified PG. All you need to know before you go is: will it be so scary that I embarrass myself by hiding under seat (in the case of *moi*, this even applied to Walt Disney films until recently)? or will it be so violent I throw up into hot date's popcorn? Etck. Neither of these is advisable on a date, although a little tremor of fear can do wonders for canoodling possibilities as long as the slashing'n'burning on screen isn't too distracting.

CONTRACEPTION

This should be the Biggest Worry of all to Teenage
Worriers with the slightest hope – or fear – of ever
actually Doing It. But since many of you who
haven't even held hands yet will think it's light
years away, take El Chubb's advice: It can happen
before you know it and you should be prepared. The
number of single parents is rising and, arrrrg, over
70,000 are Teenagers!

25

Your questions answered by Auntie Letty:

I'm under 16. Can a doctor or nurse refuse to give me contraception?
They *can* but it's quite unlikely. They may suggest you talk to your parents, but they won't make you. If a doctor does refuse, go to a family planning centre. NB Remember to ask, though. They won't give you contraception if you just say you've got a sore throat and hang about looking hopeful.

But supposing they tell my family?
They won't. Doctors *have* to keep everything you tell them confidential.

Supposing my folks find out?
They'll be more likely to be happy to find a pack of contraceptives than a little bundle of joy . . .
Anyway, they had to do stuff like this themselves once, and were worried *their* folks might find out.
Try jogging their memories or even (gasp) talking to them.

Won't it wreck the ROMANCE of Sex?
Not as much as a baby, or an STD (Sexually Transmitted Disease) will . . .

Isn't there ANY way I can get by without using contraception?
YES! Be a lesbian! (Gay boyz shld use condoms, despite no fear of pregnancy). Or, stay a virgin! Or, there's lots you can do without actually Doing It and it is Auntie Letty's advice to experiment with lots of fun before you actually have sex. But you have to be careful; it's easy (so I'm told, ahem) to get carried away, and possible, sadly, to get pregnant without full intercourse.

So what's the best thing to use?
You've got to choose. Only two types – the female condom and the male condom – actually protect you against STDs (Sexually Transmitted Diseases) like the HIV virus, which can lead to AIDS. The male condom is a V. Effective protection and can also be bought in supermarkets, chemists, Etck so it's worth

everyone having some of these. You also need to use them properly, which does not just mean to put them on willy rather than nose Etck, but remembering to read the leaflet thoroughly.

Other kinds include different kinds of pill (almost 100% effective in stopping pregnancy), diaphragm (sometimes called cap, but do not attempt to use on head unless being interviewed for fashion design course), implants, IUDs (devices inserted by a doctor into yr womb) and, V. recently, a male pill. Family planning centres give V. Good advice and leaflets on all of these (see details at end of buke). So, don't get drunk, have sex and THEN read a leaflet. Take Auntie Chubb's advice and BE PREPARED.

NB There is an *Emergency Contraception* you can take if you think you've slipped up. You have to take these pills within 72 hours at the latest, so ring Doc or go to clinic straight away.

DOUBLE DATING

Double dating is when four of you all go out together. It is a V. Good way of taking the heat, embarrassment, nerves, Worry, anxiety, stress, anguish, agitation (*that's enough adjectives — Ed.*) out of dating. F'rinstance, if all you can think of to say is 'what's your favourite colour?' you can just keep quiet and let three other people do the talking. Sadly, the only double date I've been on was with Hazel. This didn't work for the following reasons:

a) Both boyz spent whole evening drooling after her and ignoring *moi*.

b) She told them she was V. Sorry, but she only fancied gurlz and had only come on the date to cheer me up.

Hazel & moi: on blind double date... (if boy had been blind, I might have done better)

I wished she hadn't revealed her true nachure to them at this point as it made me feel even more plain, thick, ugly, dumb Etck. Bear this in mind if you are going on a double date and choose someone who is not most beautiful, desirable gurl in world as your partner.

Delilah

'Temptress, seductive and wily woman.' Sounds just like *moi* or how *moi* would be if only I had curves, bazooms Etck. But Delilah got revenge on Samson by cutting off all his wig and I would never betray Adam that way. I might feed him up a bit on V. Fattening, Pluke-Generating foods, though, so he would be less attractive to any other Delilahs he might meet. But suppose I didn't like him any more after that? Gnash, confusion, which way to go Etck?

Eve

According to ye Holey Bible, Eve was the Mother of the Human Race. Clearly, the first woman didn't have to know much about ROMANCE, since if you were the only gurl in the world and there was only one boy, you'd be almost bound to Do It together sooner or later especially since there were not yet any magazines to read instead (or football on the telly).

And I doubt Adam (that name again – swoooooon) had to think much about flowers and chocolates, or even nuts and beetles. Contraception might have been a more useful thing for Eve to know about, since one of her sons wound up killing the other, but obviously this was one bit of knowledge she didn't get when she bit that apple.

FETISHES

Seedy adults are prone to fetishes, which are described as abnormal (whatever that means) stimulants to sexual desire such as, I suppose, only being able to get an erection if you are coated in strawberry jam and beaten with rolled-up copies of the *Parliamentary Times*. Frankly, I am still young enough to think such things are V.V. UnROMANTIC and hope they are many eons away from *moi*, but then I used to get excited at just the brush of Adam's sleeve against mine. Phew, cold shower.

FIRSTS

In ROMANCE stakes, these can roughly be honed down to:

First Impression
That laser-beam of sexual dynamism that crosses a room and makes your eyes pop out on stalks like in the cartoons. Sometimes, it's followed by *an approach*. The approach usually passes on to yr best friend, who he asks out. You get *his* best frend, who closely resembles a vole. However, 'vole' is an

anagram of 'love' and if this were a story, you and the vole would walk off into sunset. In real life you spurn luckless pining vole to search for another love at-first-sight type. Same thing happens all over again.

(Feb 29)

First Date
This is the one you spend five years looking forward to, five weeks building up to, five days sorting out what to wear for, five hours getting ready for, five minutes taking everything off and putting on your usual clothes for (so that you look like you haven't bothered) and five seconds on the phone when he/she rings to say they can't make it. Other scenarios include waiting outside cinema, club, bus station Etck for three hours in hailstorm refusing to believe you have been jilted. What runs through your head at such moments is: 'He must have said an hour later, silly me'. 'He forgot to put the clock forward/back two weeks ago.' 'He's been knocked down.' (And he doesn't get up again, remaining horizontal in the arms of Tania Melt).

When you finally do get to go on a date, try to be yourself. This can be difficult, if you have no idea who that is. But if you spend the whole evening being someone else, your lurved one will wonder where you have gone. Remember, if he/she doesn't like the person you at least most resemble, he/she would not have asked you out. Remember to listen to your lurved one as well as attempting to captivate

33

him/her with your dazzling wit Etck. Dazzling wit can lead to headaches. If you get that feeling that your twin souls have only been waiting for this moment to fly, tweeting and swooping, into each others' nests, this date will be likely to end with the . . .

First Kiss

Mine, as many readers will know, was with Brian Bolt, when I scratched my nose on his specs. Since then I have had a dazzling encounter with Daniel (argh! Betrayal! Revenge!) and something even better, including a fondle, from Adam. I was V. Worried about how to kiss, but I must tell you, dear reader, that although it was a disaster with Brian, it seemed to come naturally with the other two, especially – swoon, sob – with Adam. Teenage Worriers always put *How to Kiss* as a Big Worry, but, although I worried about little else for years, I was amazed how easy it was. See also KISSING.

Am I the first boy you've ever kissed?

Not sure... you certainly LOOK like him...

Refusal to take the First Kiss any further (no contraceptives, do not know this person from Adam – sigh – told parents I'd be back two hours ago, V. Scared of Rising Feelings, Need Time to Think Etck) is bound to follow, as, some days later, will your . . .

First Tiff
Which, depending on how far relationship has progressed, leads to returning of letters, lurve tokens, storms of tears, recriminations Etck Etck. This is different from BREAKING UP, see earlier, as it is accompanied by much pashione: you vow never to have anything to do with each other ever again, and for two whole days you keep this promise. Since you still lurve each other, however, one of you is bound to crack, which leads to *First Reconciliation* and possibly, eventually, in far distant future when you have been canoodling for at least two years (this is a family buke) *First Actual Doing It*. Help, Worry, see SEX, CONTRACEPTION Etck.

FUDGE

No ROMANCE in the life of El Chubb is complete without juicy, subtle, crunchy, melting . . . fudge. No day is complete without fudge either, but if you wanted to woo *moi* then a bag of vanilla fudge would get you further than a bunch of roses. I mention this because

1) I hope my readers might send me any spare fudge they get, as long as not sampled first, and

2) Knowing what your lurved one really lurves is half the battle in the ROMANCE stakes.
F'rinstance, why take Sharon Sharalike to an arty French movie when she'd prefer a ringside seat at the all-women mud wrestling championship?

GAYS

Are you gay? If so, you may feel alone but I promise you you are not. I've often pondered that no-one seems to be worried particularly if they fancy the opposite sex from themselves, but if they fancy the same sex they often feel rising panic, want to deny it, daren't tell their frendz, family, teachers Etck. In fact, it is just as normal to be gay as it is to be heterosexual, but less common. It is also slightly less common to have red or blond hair than brown hair but no-one thinks these things are abnormal.

The trouble with schools and other Teenage Worriers and the Big Werld Outside is that there is still a lot of prejudice out there and people still joke about gays and lesbians as though they couldn't possibly be one themselves. A lot of people are so scared of admitting they might be that they even get married and have kids before they do admit it,

Q: Which of these boyz is gay? (answer on page 68)

thus making four or five people V. Unhappy. Being Gay as a Teenage Worrier is therefore more difficult than being 'straight' (which is hard enough) and it's V. Important to be able to find other gay Teenage Worriers so you can have a good old Worry together.

Although I don't fancy gurlz myself, I sometimes have a sneaky feeling I might be happier that way, as we'd have so much more in common . . . but Hazel is still V. Shy about it and hasn't told her parents that she's a lesbian yet, which I think is a shame. As far as ROMANCE goes, the story is V. similar for gay Teenage Worriers – full of hope, lust, heartbreak Etck.

There are V. Few people who haven't ever felt a little bit ROMANTIC about someone of the same sex as themselves, so if you have these feelings just be open about them and wait and see what happens. You may fancy one, both or either sex as a Teenage Worrier and this will change as you get older, until you are sure which you prefer. Society will always push you one way, so heed El Chubb's advice and Listen to your Inner Voice. If you do what your inner voice tells you, you are much likelier to end up with Mr or Ms Right in the end.

One V. imp point is that if you have a frend who is Gay, it doesn't mean that they will fancy YOU. Lots of boyz and gurlz get worried about this, or think they may be thought gay themselves if they hang out with a Gay pal. It is very Sad to think someone cld lose frendz this way so don't let yrself be stoopid about it . . .

Paranoia can wreck yr life. Gay or straight,
don't make assumptions.

GRAPES

Always have a bunch handy, so you can lie back
with Rose between teeth (as long as Rose doesn't
object, arf arf, yeech) and snarl in husky, vamp-ish
tones: 'Peel me a grape.'

GURLZ

If, to gurlz, boyz are aliens from another werld then
it follows that if you are a boy, gurlz are similarly
from another planet. However, as I pointed out in
BOYZ, earlier, gurlz are actually far more like boyz
than
  a) they like to admit
  b) boyz like to admit
  c) anything else around.
Even the old idea that boyz like looking at dirty
magazines Etck while gurlz just dream of
ROMANCE (sigh) seems to be less true now we
have unemployed gasfitters becoming strip artists
Etck, and gurlz fearlessly paying to watch them
show off their bits.
  There is a general feeling among Teenage
Worriers that gurlz are more 'mature' than boyz.
But I ask you, is reading *Smirk*, or giggling over
Weenybop any more grown-up than getting excited

over *Turbo-Anorak Weekly* or *Megatit*? Is plastering your walls with pix of Brad Pitpony significantly more mature than putting up Melinda Bazoom? Is painting each finger and toenail a different pattern of silver, purple, lime green Etck any cleverer than fart-lighting?

However, one important thing that still separates the gurlz from the boyz, is that gurlz can be mothers. Being a mother also stays a BIG WISH for lots of gurlz whereas it is rare to find a boy who is longing to be a dad . . . This may make gurlz more ROMANTIC and lead them to spend time thinking how they are going to get a family.

Resist it, dear gurlz, until you are well past being a Teenage Worrier. Get a contraception and an education. Cos that prince may not come and you will have to earn a living, even if he does too. You do not want to wind up selling spotty bod on streets or dressing your five-year-old up as a baby to tempt passers-by to chuck you a few pence . . .

Hay ^AAAAChoo?

A Roll in the hay was what Rural lurvers did. Sounds V. prickly to *moi* but preferable, as long as not highly allergic, to bike shed, urban wasteground Etck.

Holiday Romances

You are walking on tropical beach, wearing just a
shimmer of polyester temptation, your hair blowing
lightly against your radiant tan. Suddenly, you feel a
soft burning down your back. Surely you put on
your factor 2000 lotion on top of your fake-tanning-
cream? You are a Worrier, after all, and do not want
skin cancer. But no, the burn you feel is the searing
glance of – Donatello Machismo. This dazzling
stranger, a symphony of sinews complete with natty
designer swimwear, mutters softly 'Are these yours?'
proferring an elegant pair of, wait for it, designer
sunglasses. 'N-no,' you stutter shyly, allowing your
fawn-like eyes to gleam softly beneath the fronds of
your newly washed, eloquently tousled mane. 'But I
wouldn't mind if they were,' you add, with a look
pregnant with meaning and so far little else, as he
slips his golden arm round your slender waist and
moves with you, as one, into the sparkling azure
foam that eternally breaks against the silver sand.
Ten days of bliss are followed by ten months of
wondering why you never heard from him again.
Surely, how could you? But surely? You gave him
the wrong address? He must even now be working
night and day to raise the air fare (funny, he said his
dad owned a fleet of aeroplanes). And so on. You
plot to return to the same place. If you are lucky

enough to get there, you will be tragically confronted, on your first day, by the sight of Donatello, approaching another sylph, proferring the pair of elegant designer sunglasses which he always carries especially for that purpose.

I'd go to the Ends of the Earth for you

But would you STAY there?

Even with this tragick ending, we all dream of a holiday ROMANCE like the one above. Better two weeks of passion, we think, than none at all. But if other Worriers are remotely like *moi*, then the nearest we will come will be a wet afternoon in Bognor with Kevin Snoad, who treated me to two games in the amusement arcade and half a bag of chips before trying to insist on a quickie behind the pier.

Britain is not a great place for holiday ROMANCE. And whatever the venue, the result is always the same: you write eight long letters and are lucky to get a postcard. If you do, it says: *Hope your OK. Im fine. Met a great new bird in magaluf. Kevin.*

INFATUATION

Is when you get obsessed with somebody, usually someone you have only just glimpsed and never talked to – and you just can't stop thinking about them. Ye film star Brad Pitpony has this effect on *moi*, or did have, as now I am fifteen I have thrown away such childish dreams in order to search for the True Meaning of ROMANCE. However, it is possible to be infatuated with the boy/gurl-next-door or whatever and it can be V. Painful when you linger about hoping to bump into them casually and they pass by as if you were but a flea. They don't do this to be mean but simply because, sadly, they have failed to notice your existence. If they *have* noticed you, because you have taken care to send them ill-disguised Valentines, lurve notes Etck or because you gaze at them with doggy affection whenever they appear, they will probably feel flattered. If you push it, though, they will feel cheesed off. If they are Nasty (sadly, objects of infatuation can be nasty) they may take advantage of you and then reject you. It is better to be infatuated from afar, as real ROMANCE can only happen when both people are involved and really no-one sensible wants to go out with someone who hangs on their every werd and drools as if they were a deity. If anyone did that to you, you'd think they were a few crumbs short of a slice of bread, wouldn't you?

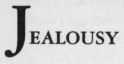

JEALOUSY

The green-eyed monster. Why is it called that?
Why *green* with envy? Why not blue? Or red? El
Chubb's theory of colour cannot help but make her
wonder why the colour of grass, trees and natural
planties should be associated with the corkscrewing
sense of overpowering dume you feel when yr
beLurved walks off with someone much cleverer,
prettier, wittier, sportier Etck Etck than you.

Look – I don't want any strings, OK?

How about CHAINS?

However, it is a monster which attacks all of us from
time to time (*moi*, most of the time). You feel its
fiery tendrils when the object of your affection

objects to your affections and flings his arse (sorry, arms) around Tania Melt instead. The worst kind of jealousy though is not when you are wishing you could go out with someone and feeling dead jealous of the people who *are* going out with them – it is the jealousy you feel when you are with someone and think they might be seeing someone else. This is how I have felt on two occasions with Daniel and on one with Adam. I still lie awake nights just wondering who he lurves, now he is in Los Angeles (sigh).

The only ways you can deal with jealousy are:

a) Try not to feel it in the first place. This involves becoming a Buddhist and learning not to want.

3) Standing outside house of beLurved and howling like banshee. This involves unacceptable loss of dignity.

E) Locking self in room and sobbing until someone (probably yr poor old mum) comes to show they care.

F) BUT the most sensible (who ever said Teenage Worriers were sensible?) thing to do would be to realize that if your rival is preferred to you, then you can't be happy with this lurve object in the first place. If they are stupid enough just to like her because she sings like lark, has hair like angel, bazooms of sex goddess Etck then they are not classy enough to appreciate what's specially you, commune meaningfully with yr Soul Etck.

KISSING (part two thousand and forty one)

The reason many Teenage Worriers Worry so much about how to Kiss, is they are scared they will blow the Big Moment of the First Kiss, by producing

A) V. wet slobbery ones that make the recipient feel they have been leapt on by V. friendly, ancient dog

B) V. Dry rasping ones that sandpaper a few layers off beLurved's luscious lips; not opening mouth wide enough so teeth collide, doing untold damage that will mean centuries in the dentist's torture chamber, negotiating complicated co-production with bank, National Lottery Etck

C) Opening mouth too wide and finding it full of beLurved's nose and chin

D) Missing target altogether and ending up with mouthful of leather jacket

E) Being unable to breathe while kissing and therefore emitting noise like drowning rodent OR having to stop at high point in order to breathe in lungfuls of fresh mountain air (unlikely if venue is alley behind dustbins, or *Le Club Tarantulla*).

Is this the first time you've kissed a girl?

In daylight, yes...

I've long argued that kissing shld be on National Curriculum. I spot a gap in the Market. If you can't get it on the school curriculum, why not go Private? If you know any V. sinuous sexperienced people, why not suggest they put an ad in their local paper offering sex tuition and kissing lessons to Teenage Worriers? Naturally I am not talking about seedy types who offer ads for demolishing temporary erections, or offering large white chests with no drawers for sale. I am talking about V. Kind people who would TEACH, but not take advantage. Am I an innocent abroad?

But kissing does come naturally with someone you like – it does, *really*, as I have discovered with Adam (moan gnash, tragic demeanour, will I ever feel like that again, Etck). However much I say this, though, you don't believe *moi*, so here, at last, are El

Chubb's definitive kissing tips. **Please read once, then never again**, otherwise you will keep thinking: Have I missed out Stage One? What comes next? Etck. Then the whole point of kissing will be lost . . .

ESSENTIAL KISSING TIPS

<u>KISSING TIP</u> (No.468): Do <u>NOT</u> arrange mouth in kissing position until in close proximity to Lurve object, for fear of dissuading same.

1. Make sure you are warm. A cold nose in the eye and chapped lips do little for passion.
2. Relax. Think hot maple syrup.
3. Trace shape of beLurved's lips with finger.
4. Murmur sweet nothing.
5. Rub your cheek against beLurved's cheek. (Make sure you use face.)

6. If yr beLurved has a wisp of hair floating across face, take it gently between yr lips and move it to side (this was a V.Seductive trick of Adam's and I writhe to think he might be doing this with Another as I write). But naturally harder with partner who has Afro or crew cut.

7. Move lips slowly towards beLurved's. Hover.

8. Draw back a moment to whisper another sweet nothing.

9. Place lips (closed) on beLurved's.

10. Purse lips and move them about. Open them V. Slightly.

11. Phew. Kiss then continues in variety of ways, the best of which is that beLurved moves tip of tongue into yr mouth and your tongue then connects with your beLurved's. I hope BOYZ are reading this cos they cld do with a few tips from Daniel Hope. After which whole business gets hungry, steamy Etck. I cannot prescribe future moves cos it takes a minimum of two people to make a good kiss and you can't be sure what each of them will do next. What I can say, is if you want to build up good head of steam, then keep it all V. SLOW.

Er, and DON'T do anything you don't want to do or are not prepared for. A boy f'rinstance who wants to take it further but has 'forgotten' his condoms is a boy Not Worth Bothering About. Here endeth first lesson in kissing. Now put self in ice bucket and forget about it until you are twenty-one.

51

LEAP YEAR

This is supposed to be the time when a gurl can propose marriage to a boy, but nowadays I hope liberated Teenage Worriers have no fear of proposing in any year (except normal fear of millstones round neck, life of domestic glume Etck).

LOVE LETTERS

These, like poems, are the most composed and least read of all Teenage Worriers' outpourings. Who among you has not lain awake imagining a letter they will send to their beLurved, only to realize, as the chill dawn stretches its clammy fingers Etck, that you simply don't have the courage. And what about the letters that you get? No-one can write one nearly as good as the one in your imagination . . .

V. sad point of Teenage Worriers' lives in 21st century may be final end of love letter flapping hopefully through letter-box as e.mail dot.com may overtake all handwritten stuff.

However, even if you are all wired up for e.mail, it is good to know how to write a love letter. A few well-chosen werds have V. Powerful effect.

1) Speling it more or less write is going two help. Yore trew luv may think yew stoopid if yew

Embarrassing envelope.

Unspeakably embarrassing envelope. Avoid at all costs.

cant spel. Thiss iz not nessessarilee trew, but a bak-
to-baysix noshiun that has cort onn, even amung
Teenage wurriers.

2) If you are serious, do not embarrass the
recipient by scrawling hearts all over envelope. Also,
do not write S.W.A.L.K. (sealed with a loving kiss)
or 'Hurry postman don't be slow, this is for my
Romeo' on the back. Your true lurve probably has a
younger sibling who will tease him or her
mercilessly at the sight of such stuff.

3) Say something about the time you last met,
that will feel special. Something original, like *I love
the way your mouth goes up at the corners even when you
aren't smiling*. Or *I never thought an anorak could look
OK with dreadlocks, but you've taught me different*, or
something.

LUST

Lust is strong fizzical attraction, often confused with
'fancying'. But fancying someone and lusting after
them are subtly different, as 'fancying' implies
actually liking them a bit whereas 'lust' is more,
ahem, rampant. It makes you feel: *cor, phew, sweat,
pant, don't-care-what-they're-really-like-just-got-to-have-
'em*. If boy approaches you in such a way, yell 'NO'
and run. Unless, of course, you feel the same.

MARRIAGE

L. Chubb sez: Teenage Worriers should not get married. Course, if you want to tie knot when V. Old, like 25, then V. nice (wish own parents had got married, might have made me more secure, Etck. Sob).

L. Chubb nose ring. → Put it on yr Lurved one's Hooter and LEAD them around.

Monogamy

Although if you believed the newspapers you would think Teenage Worriers were at it like rabbits with every available passing person, most of us are V.V. ROMANTIC and, when you are ROMANTICally in love, you cannot imagine ever being with anyone else, so monogamy is an essential part of ROMANCE.

Even if I do have more than one love affair I am sure I will turn out to be at the very least a serial monogamist as I can't even talk to more than one boy at once.

Naughty Bits

Victorian times are past — when men swooned with fright when they discovered their wives didn't have willies, or did have pubic hair, or whatever it was — and now we all know better. But DO we? After years of giggling at the mention of bums, willies Etck and making rude noises to annoy grown-ups, deep embarrassment descends during the Teenage Worrier years at the thought of any Naughty Bit being mentioned in front of any adults. If you have reached this stage, you have probably started Worrying about your own Naughty Bits. These

Worries are usually concerned with shape, size, angle, or lack. The overwhelming question is: Are my naughty bits Normal?

The almost certain answer to this question is, yes.

Teenagers lie awake Worrying they might be different from everyone else and have no idea what size or shape their bits shld actually be. Well, kids, you're right. We are *all* different and no willy or vagina is exactly the same, so there. Sexual development also starts at very different times so there's no point in a thirteen-year-old gurl or boy even thinking about how small their willy or bazooms are until they are five years older. That's just the way it is. Not that it stops me Worrying about my miniscule bazooms, but at least it helps to know others are in the same *bâteau*.

The point, ahem, of Naughty Bits in ROMANTIC terms, is that they are Focal Points (that werd again) for seething pashioncs Etck. This is why it is a V.Good idea to keep them under wraps if you are keen not to go too far. Don't ever make the mistake of thinking your bazooms are so small that no-one will like them. Or too big, either.

I would like to start a fashion for a new naughty bit. I would choose the earlobe, since earlobes are V. sensitive to nibbling Etck and could become just as naughty, with a little encouragement, as the bazoom. Also, they are freely available to both sexes. Ear lobe covers would be a must, in a variety of gorgeous fabrics and colourways – appliquéd, sequinned, whatever. Then, on hot summer days, we could all walk around naked except for our lobe covers. This would cheer up everyone who is Worried about their current naughty bits, cos no-one would pay any attention to willies or bazooms any more and all attention would be focused on the LOBE.

As all imaginative Teenage Worriers will have noted, those with tiny lobes, or lugs like taxi doors, would suffer.

N<small>o</small>

V. Imp accessory for the ROMANTICally inclined, as a 'no' said early will prevent all kinds of future heartbreak.

A famous myth is that *'No doesn't always mean no.'* Oh, yes it does.

No no NO! No! No!
No No! No! No!
No!
NO!
No no NO! No!
NO! No No no NO!
No! No!
NO
No!
No no NO!
NO!
Er, I'll take that as a no, then?

There will always be a few tragic boyz who think that, while a gurl knows what 'yes' and 'no' mean in everyday English, she means something completely different if she's talking about sex. If a gurl says no, and a boy forces her to have sex, this is rape. No-one ever ever *ever* has to have sex unless they want to. Don't *ever* feel guilty for saying no.

And, if someone says 'no' to you, just accept it. You can always try again later, to see if they've changed their mind.

El Chubb's TIP: practise chatting up boyz from age of twelve. Try it espesh on the V. handsome, world-weary ones who are bound to say *Non* and then you will not weep and moan and pull your hairs out one by one in anguish if Turned Down later when you really mean it, as you will be quite used to handling it.

NB Have plan ready if someone you don't like accepts and thinks this means they can have their wicked way with you. eg: 'I was only practising', 'I thought you were somebody else', 'I thought I was somebody else', Etck Etck.

Orgasm

Also known as 'coming' (and sadly, often a prelude to boy going), this is the big bit of overwhelming Feeling (surge, throb, choirs of birdies, clash of cymbals, raging waterfalls Etck) you get at the culmination of ye sexual act, or while doing things to your own Naughty Bits. Some V. Romantic people think you can get an orgasm just by looking at the one you feel V. ROMANTIC about, but even I, with all my seething pashiones, flowing juices Etck, find this hard to believe.

PHEROMONES

Obviously, these little chemical attractants have been working on the human race for centuries, without our even knowing it. They doubtless made the pharoahs moan, too, and perhaps that's how they got their name.

PORNOGRAPHY

Pheromones →
(or fleas?)

This is a word that sends parents running screaming. The idea that their offspring might have rude pictures of gurlz or boyz stuffed under their pillow is too much for them. BUT, although there is horrible pornography, there is also a lot of stuff that most boyz are bound to look at some time or another — and it seems to be catching on for gurlz too.

See Naughty Pix
on next Page →
(if you move FAST)

The main prob with these pix is they don't look like many real gurlz, ie: they have vast bazooms, curves where most of us have dents, and dents where most of us have big fat roly bits. The gurlz who pose for them often got their bits from a plastic sturgeon (sorry, surgeon) and I find it V. Tragick waste of human potential that this is all they can think to do with their life.

And then she RIPPED the flimsy covering to reveal, a LONG, FIRM, GLISTENING bar of fudge

Whatever turns you on...

One thing you can say about any kind of porn is that it's definitely not ROMANTIC.

PREGNANCY

The scene is a candlelit fast-food joint. A beautiful Teenage Worrier is stirring her milkshake, with a wistful, dreamy, faraway look in her soulful eyes. There are no burgers because of the power cut. It is freezing cold. But she is warmed by a secret knowledge. She can't wait to tell Clint Cleft, the Love-of-her-life, the marvellous news. The door opens and an icy blast from the freezing mean streets of the throbbing urban jungle blows in. And so does Clint Cleft. They have known each other for six whole months and now she knows that soon they will be as ONE. Clint approaches, his boyish smile decorating his manly chops, his long limbs purposeful, blah blah . . .

Gurl: Darling, I've got some wonderful news.
Clint: Oh good. I'm glad you're happy, because there's something I want to tell you, too.
Gurl: Don't you want to know what it is?
Clint: No, that's fine, as long as you're pleased, because . . .
Gurl: There are no longer two of us in this relationship, sweetheart, there are three.
Clint: But I know. That's what I was going to tell you. I'm SO pleased you don't mind.
Gurl: How did you know? I've only just found out myself. And why should I mind?
Clint: Well, you know, I thought you'd be jealous.
Gurl: Jealous? Of our little baby?
Clint: Well, I wouldn't exactly call Gloria Scroggins a *baby* – I mean, she's got whopping . . .
Gurl: Gloria Scroggins! What's Gloria Scroggins got to do with it?
Clint: But you just said you *knew*. I've been seeing her for about a month . . .
Gurl: Boooo hoooo. Sob. Monster. Etck.

This tragic scenario is played up and down the country every day. So is another, involving the dreadful panic of late periods, over-the-counter pregnancy tests, huge relief, huger despair. Those ads that say a puppy is not just for Christmas, but for life, would be better applied to babies, since around 100,000 Teenagers a year become pregnant

ACCIDENTS
CAUSE
PEOPLE

and most of these are unplanned. It really is the most important thing of all to check out and use contraception before you get near sex, because by the time you are near, you may find yourself actually Doing It and then it will be Too Late. Arg, squirm, cling to virginity as to life-belt in raging ocean Etck.

PRUDERY

Is when people are V. Disapproving of sex and do not like to admit it is taking place. When the Victorians covered piano-legs in lace knickers, it was a sign of prudery. Although if they thought Men wld get excited and mount the piano, maybe they had a rather exaggerated view of the carnal instinct after all. Prudery usually leads to hypocrisy and people turning blind eyes, telling fibs Etck to keep harmony. Alternatively, it can just be a sign that sex is not your cup of tea and that your cup of tea is more likely to be – a cup of tea. Why not?

QUESTIONS

ROMANTIC QUESTIONS: EL CHUBB'S LIST
Write the numbers 1,2,3,4 in any order several times, on piece of paper. This is yr special personal chart. Choose a question and then close your eyes and wave your finger around before stabbing it down on chart. Then look up answer, ie: if you score a 2 for question B, you look up B2.
A) Does the object of my desire lurve me?
B) Does the one I am thinking of think of me as much as I think of them?
C) Is the thing that I dread going to happen?

D) Has he/she done it as many times as they say?

E) Will I be a virgin for long?

F) Will my nose/bazooms/willy get any bigger?

Answers

a1) Yes a2) Much more than you think a3) More than you love them a4) Why? Do you lurve them?

B1) Far more B2) Nearly B3) Depends what you mean by 'think' B4) Ask them

C1) Never C2) Depends how good your contraception was C3) Nothing as bad as you dread will happen C4) No

D1) More D2)No, they haven't done it at all D3) Not quite D4) Exactly

E1) As long as you choose E2) Ages E3) Six years, ten months, one week, four days and two hours E4) No

F1) No, smaller F2) Yes, much F3) So big you'll need to get doors specially widened if you go in sideways F4) Exactly the right size

Tips for analysing oracle

If you believe a single word of any of the above replies, you are V. Gullible. How could *moi* possibly know anything about you? F'rinstance, how could the answers: E3) or F3) possibly be true? The same is obviously true of all the other answers only, like those daft quizzes in magazines like *Smirk* and *Yoo Hoo*, they are more cleverly disguised and give the appearance of TRUTH: beware quizzes, gentle reader.

RED ROSES

Still best ROMANTIC gift. Cheapest, too, if you have any growing, since flowers from own garden or windowbox still most ROMANTIC of all. Do not, however, confuse geraniums with roses; geraniums do not pick well.

Arg. He gave me Hemlock...

The Language of FLOWERS

Answer to question on page 37

A: V. sorry, but can't remember whether ALL of the boyz are gay, or NONE of them. Never mind, eh?

SEASONS

Winter: What cld be more ROMANTIC than a snowy stroll, mufflers entwined, throwing crumbs to swans as they glide along icy lakeside? Even the scarlet nose of yr companion, complete with frozen drip, cannot detract from Winter's paradise . . .

Spring: is ye traditional season for ROMANCE. What cld be more ROMANTIC than a Spring stroll, patting the curly heads of bouncy lambs who bleat their cheerful bleats as they Spring through cowslips, primroses Etck? Even as you slip on cowpats, you may clutch the hand of your belurved...

Summer: nothing, surely, cld be more ROMANTIC than a hot, hazy, stroll along a golden beach, entwined in the strong arms of . . . Etck. (But see HOLIDAY ROMANCES for, um, downside.)

Autumn: season of mists and mellow nostalgia much belurved of teenage Worriers. What cld be more ROMANTIC than wandering through crackling leaves, the smell of bonfires in your hooter? So what if you are wandering alone; the season itself will instill you with all the same feeling you get with ROMANCE: melancholy, longing, yearning, shivering, unspeakable glume Etck, Etck.

☼ ☁ The Romance ☁ ☼

Ah! Ye Romance of WINTER: Season of Red roses,
I mean, noses.

Bless the Sexy SPRING, as it brings Hay Fever.

of the Seasons

The sultry SUMMER: season of SWEAT.

Turn over a new leaf and FALL for someone in Autumn.

SEX

When middle-aged Worriers think about their own
dear little Teenage Worriers having sex, they
tremble with trepidation. This is because middle-
aged Worriers remember their own mis-spent yoof
and although they wish they had mis-spent a bit
more of it they are scared their own offspring will be
Doing It all the time and fail their exams, have
babies, get STDs (sexually transmitted diseases)
Etck, Etck. What many of them have forgotten is
how Worried they were about Sex themselves and
how little of it they actually did. This is still true of
Teenage Worriers today. Apparently the average age
for first having sex is seventeen. Since people always
lie about such things, this is quite likely to make
the average age older. Also it could mean that even
those who are Doing It at seventeen have only done
it once. Even if all seventeen-year-olds did it several
times a week (V.V. Unlikely, where would they
go?), it still means that loads of other people have
sex for the first time much later (and that doesn't
count all the people who never have it at all . . .).

ROMANCE is V. Obvious prelude to SEX, but
there doesn't have to be much sex at all in a
ROMANCE, which can be a meeting of minds, or a
brushing of fingertips, and still take up a bigger
proportion of your heart, mind, head Etck than

72

outrageous nooky with someone you're not that interested in as a person. There's lots of pressure to get off with people as a Teenage Worrier. You don't have to. Wait till you really like someone. In my case, sadly, the people I really like always get off with someone else, sob. But perhaps one day . . . yearn.

Kissing, cuddling and canoodling are all part of sex and you are having a sexual relationship if you are doing any of these – *and* it's much safer than full intercourse.

Meanwhile, here are El Chubb's answers to just some of the Sex Worries y'all have sent moi :

DON'T CONDOMS WRECK ROMANCE?

Opposite, obviously is true. STDs, pregnancies and endless Worry Etck wreck it, seriously. I have been carrying a pack of three condoms around ever since I can remember, but sadly I have never had the chance to offer them to my beLurved in moment of high pashione. (Must check their sell-by date.)

HE/SHE SEZ THEY WON'T GO OUT WITH ME UNLESS I DO IT. SO SHOULD I?

Pressure is not Romance. Your reply: get lost, sucker, plenty more fish in ocean Etck. (NB, although yr personal ocean may currently seem polluted and fish-free, you still have to think this way. Another bus *will* come along eventually.)

I'M SCARED IT MIGHT HURT AND THERE'LL BE LOADS OF BLOOD.
V.V.V.V. Unlikely. See also VIRGINITY.

WILL HE/SHE THINK LESS OF ME IF WE DO IT?
It has been known for a gurl to sleep with her dreamboat only to hear that dreaded werd *'slag'*. If such a boy is your dreamboat, could be you need a brain transplant. Check him OUT, then chuck him out.

IF WE HAVE SEX, WILL EVERYONE KNOW?
No. Having sex does not cause your Bits to glow in the dark, or change your fizzical appearance in any way. So unless you or your partner spray-paint the lavvies or tattoo your foreheads with the message 'We've dunnit', no-one will know. An element of mutual trust is obviously useful.

IF SOMEONE SEEMS TO HAVE DONE IT WITH LOTS OF PEOPLE, SURELY THAT MEANS THEY'LL DO IT WITH ME?
Arggg. Are any of you this stoopid? You know YOU wouldn't just do it with anyone, so why should someone else? And would you WANT to do it with someone who does it with everyone?

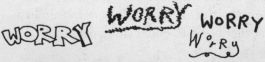

I'M 22 AND I HAVEN'T DONE IT. DOES THIS MEAN I'M A WIMP?

This wd usually be a question asked by a boy, since gurlz who do it later are, unfairly, never called wimps, but put on pedestals Etck. Yawn. But boyz, as well as gurlz, should wait till they're ready to do it with someone they really like. Such a boy wld get more respeck from *moi*, I know that (gnash, moan, is Adam doing it with Another?).

SOFA

Yes! If you do not have a trew lurve with whom to be ROMANTIC, a sofa is a great replacement. Sofas are warm and cuddly, let you lie full length on them whenever you want without complaining and never disagree with a word you say. (Once you do get a ROMANCE going, introduce him or her to your sofa as soon as possible, har har leer.)

Telephone

My Adored Father's inability to pay a telephone bill on time means that for about half the year our phone is cut off. This is a tragick disadvantage when it comes to ROMANCE. Just when I am longing to whisper melting sweet nothings into eager receiver Etck, there is nothing sweet but whirr and cackle of static. However, the fact that siblings, parents Etck are picking up telephone extensions to eavesdrop or blow raspberries means that most ROMANTIC telephone conversations are more likely to go like this:

Brrrrrrrr Brrrrrrrr

Teenage Worrier 1: Hi

Teenage Worrier 2: Hi

Teenage Worrier 1: It's me

Teenage Worrier 2: U-huh

Teenage Worrier 1: How you doing?

Teenage Worrier 2: Fine.

Teenage Worrier 1: Great.

Teenage Worrier 2: You OK?

Teenage Worrier 1: Fine.

Teenage Worrier 2: Great.

Teenage Worrier 1: yeh

Teenage Worrier 2: Well, uh, see you around

Teenage Worrier 1: yeh

Teenage Worrier 2: bye

Teenage Worrier 1: yeh

The above is a direct transcript of a Teenage Worrier's long-awaited phone call. What she went on to do immediately afterwards, was to phone three frendz in turn and discuss each element of above, ie: what did 'uh-huh' mean in the context of the conversation? How was she to interpret 'great'? The best bit, all the frendz agreed, was 'see you around' which gave great cause for hope. The fact that the BOY had phoned at all was also V. Exciting, everyone thought. Arg. Maybe it is better to have phone on blink than to be forced to endure such tortures.

TRUST

When you decide, in heat of pashione, to allow that lingering kiss to go a little further, only to find that your bra size is pinned on the school noticeboard the following day, you can bet your life your Trust has been Betrayed. Avoiding such humiliations means only snogging V. Nice trustworthy people who you like and who like you. Your intuition shld tell you who they are. NB When drunk, or under influence of other intoxicating substances, intuition is V.Blunt.

Underwear

As ROMANCE progresses (sigh), the chances are
that underwear may become visible. You do not
have to be at the stage of actually removing it to
start Worrying about it. In fact, I have been
Worrying about my own underwear since I was six
years old and realized I had to display it to the
whole class in PE lessons. Oh woe, those holes . . .
those mortifying colour combinations. My little
brother Benjy still suffers same indignity if my Only
Mother forces him to wear pants with pictures of
Timmy the tractor on . . .

Ye Boxer shorts are beating up Y-Fronts in battle
for boyz underbits.

However, if you're addicted to *Smirk*, you will be
bombarded by styles and materials. Arg. F'rinstance,
in a recent issue of *Yoo Hoo*, we could choose from
white lycra cotton vest and shorts, white lacey
v-neck T-shirt and shorts . . . silver satin vest and
brief set . . . white ribbed T-shirt with meshed
flowers (*what!*) or a blue velour T-shirt and white
heart knickers. Arg. The cheapest of these little
outfits is more than yours truly will ever see in a
month. Stay cheap and simple with . . . *Letty
Chubb's Underwear Tips*:
Keep it clean.
Keep it neat.
Keep it snowy white or sooty black.
The tragedy of the pale grey knicker that should
have been dazzlingly white can be avoided by
buying black, but black too, can turn to fog. But

wait! Is this El Chubb enslaving herself and other Teenage Worriers in the heartrending pit of *looksism*? How can a plain grey knicker be a *tragedy*? Get Real. Who cares if your knickers are beige or grey? Up with mushroom panties! Down with white panties! (whooops). Fact is, nice, neat, non-baggy underwear is appealing on both sexes so, um, I think I'll stick with convention on this one. No need for fabu-bras (nothing to put in them in the sad case of *moi*, anyway) or negligees in floaty wisps. Just clean white bits to cover your bits. Same goes for boyz and gurlz, OK? NB Boyz, no boxer shorts with naked women on them (pictures, I mean), per-leeze.

VALENTINES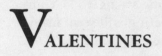

It is V. Cruel the way, year after year, Feb 14th comes round just after Feb 13th (not that I believe 13 is unlucky, but Feb 13th does make you V. Nervy and glumey) and yet it never EVER brings a Valentine from the person you're hoping to hear from. There may well be well-meaning Valentines from your aunty or little brother or even one, in my case, from Brian Bolt . . . but I know this year I will look in vain for a Los Angeles postmark . . .

I have even got my reply card ready. On the front it says: *What?? Be YOUR Valentine? You lousy no-good two-timer! And on the inside, it says: Of course . . .* But I feel it is destined to stay in my bedside table along with the other Valentines I have bought over the years and never sent. Sob, self-pity Etck.

L. CHUBB'S TIP TO CHEER UP VALENTINES DAY

Lonely Hearts Party
Ask everyone who hasn't got a boy/gurlfrend to come. Put on V.V. sad music, or a tape of rain pattering into puddles, or sound effects of wailing violins or banshees. All stand in a circle and sob loudly. Who knows? Maybe a kindly tissue will be offered to you by an intriguing stranger . . . Think how V. ROMANTIC yr meeting will seem many years from now when you are old and grey.

NB When aroused by lust and indeed by ROMANCE, the human heart beats faster. I guess this is why it is used for valentines and all other symbols of lurve. But it doesn't change half as much as the male willy does when aroused (so I am told, ahem) so why not put Big Willies on Valentine's Cards Etck? Another thing that happens is you sweat more. How about lovely big fat drops of SWEAT?

CAMPAIGN for sweaty Valentines!

Vests

string vest (nice)

L. Chubb Best vest gone west

Not most ROMANTIC of accessories (see
UNDERWEAR, earlier) but useful if you still can't
really fill a bra (sob, cringe) and don't want to reveal
whole bod during canoodling.

Virgins

Rather comforting to think that everyone has been
one of these and most Teenage Worriers, *moi*self
included, still are. I'm beginning to think it would
be nice just to Do It once, then not bother about it
again, as the Worry involved gives me sleepless
nights.

In ye olden daze it was V. Imp to be a virgin
when you married, if you were a gurl. This was so
the man wld be sure any offspring of the union were
his alone (though what stopped you from Doing It
with someone else in the afternoons I have no idea).
People were so keen to prove they were virgins that
they even had little fake bags of blood so they could
pretend their hymen (the wafer-thin covering across
the vagina) had broken on Day One of the
honeymoon. In fact, now as then, most gurlz'
hymens are broken long before they have sex, either
just by running about, or riding a bike, or anything,

and they don't even notice it. So the fear of agony, tearing and pouring bludde on your first sexshual encounter is one more Worry crossed off list (phew).

I am a grate believer, despite aforesaid worry about being a virgin, in having a ROMANTIC time the first time. It seems a bit glumey to think of a quickie behind the dustbins like poor old Rover, or a feverish snog while babysitting on a neighbour's sofa that goes too far – especially if the neighbours return in the middle and wonder why you are upside down with a hunk instead of glueing your ear to the baby alarm as you shld be . . .

For *moi*, it will be in a waterbed with Adam Stone – or Nothing (Pretty easy to guess which . . .). I s'pose I'll end up V. Proud of my virginity when I'm an old lady of thirty. In fact, I am determined to be V. Proud of it Now.

WATER

Ye ROMANCE of water! What cld be more ROMANTIC than a stroll by a moonlit lake? Or splashing in a cule pule on Californian mountainside? Or sitting by fountain (cor, spurt, Etck) in a sunny pizza, I mean piazza, listening to gentle strumming of stomach juices accompanied by gurgling of guitar?

There is an old psychology trick that asks you to think of some kind of water. Go on, do it now.

What did you think of?
Ocean means you are V. Sexy.
Sea, ditto but less.
Lake, calmly sensual.
Stream, working on it.

I always think of a dripping tap, which goes to prove such Deep Insights into Yuman condition are V. Unsound.

Let's hear it for WATER! Biggest ROMANTIC ingredient of all! (Also, if you drink same, less likely to end up in V. UnROMANTIC situation leading to regret, pining Etck.)

XCITEMENT

(OK, excitement, but I'm not doing XYLOPHONES in ROMANCE, and I've done KISSING, so there.)

What is ROMANCE without that fluttering of the heart, panting of the, er, pants, trembling of the nether regions (must check what a nether is before handing in buke) that accompanies a first date . . . or kiss. The excitement of seeing someone you really like the look of and (gulp) finding that they like the look of you too. Having checked it actually is you they're talking to (in the case of *moi*, it's usually Hazel, who is standing behind me, that has caused their eyes to light up and their willies, I mean spirits, to rise) you are now in a position to offer them your phone number. Excitement!

ROMANCE!

The next step is sitting by the phone. It rings!
Excitement!

ROMANCE!

It is for your mum. It rings again. Excitement!

ROMANCE!

It is for your dad! It rings again. Excitement!

ROMANCE!

It is your beLurved. Double Excitement!

Double ROMANCE!

Then you get all that stuff about where to meet.
Then there's the ten hours of getting ready, by
which time the excitement is at such a fever pitch
that no-one on earth could live up to your
expectations. Never mind. Excitement is what
ROMANCE is all about . . .

... which leads us to ...

YES

(ok, if you like, yeah, Yup, u-huh, mmm).

This may be the moment when you cast cares to the wind and decide to wallow in undiluted pashione. But it may equally be the time when you want to say Yes to a kiss, Yes to canoodling, but No to anything else. If ROMANCE is blossoming, this will not deter your lurve object (see SEX, earlier). And together you can waft on a sea of ROMANCE, saying Yes to all the things you both like, and even some of the things you're not crazy about but know your lurved one likes (by this, I mean consenting to watch mud-wrestling, not hanging upside down in frogman's flippers and beating yourself with a wet haddock).

However true my ROMANCE is, I will never however say Yes to fish and chips (can't stand fish).

ZITS

If a lonely zit is wandering the universe, searching for a home, it will zero in on Brian's sizeable conk even before my own. Yet even Adam has zits. And I lurve every last spot of them. So you see, although they plague the Teenage Worrier who has them, ROMANCE *can* shine through.

ENDPIECE

And now, dear reader, we end our brief stroll through the vineyards of ROMANCE. With sinking hearts, we bid farewell to the groves of grapes, eternal sunshine, sifting sands, twinkling fountains, scarlet blooms, golden summers Etck of our imagination and turn our sinking hearts once more to Sluggs Comprehensive, GCSEs, and our best chance of ROMANCE — a clash of teeth, or braces, with Syd Snogg round the corner.

And we ask ourselves: does ROMANCE really exist?

My answer, dearest reader, is yes, briefly, only to end in tears in the tragick case of moi . . . and yet, Hope does spring eternal, and even now, El Chubb is dusting herself off, writing one last heartfelt epistle to Adam Stone before brushing wig for first time in months and facing werld with Spring in Step.

Who knows who might be waiting round next corner? What sweet nothings he might murmur? True ROMANCE can lie in smallest places, in cosiest corners, in a look, in a werd . . . and we all may find it someday . . .

Yrs truly, (amid sunshine, tears, glume mixed with sprinkling of JOY Etck.)

Letty Chubb

Help!

Useful telephone numbers

CONTRACEPTION

Brook Advisory Centres
0800 018 5023 (helpline, office hours)
020 7617 8000 (recorded information helpline)
Contraceptive and counselling service for the under 25s. Local clinics throughout the UK. Under 16s can obtain confidential help.

Family Planning Association
020 7837 5432 (confidential helpline)
Clinics throughout the UK. Can also send V. helpful leaflets.

GAY/LESBIAN

Lesbian and Gay Switchboard
020 7837 7324 (24 hours, Mon to Fri
www.queery.org.uk

Advice and info service that also offers advice for friends and family. NB They are really hard to get through to, but don't give up.

North London Lesbian and Gay Project
020 7607 8346
Run the lesbian, gay and bisexual Youth Project for under 25s, and can provide advice, info and education resources.

COUNSELLING

Youth Access
020 8772 9900
Details of young people's counsellors throughout the country.

Childline
Freephone 0800 1111

The Samaritans
08457 909090

THE TEENAGE WORRIER'S POCKET GUIDE TO FAMILIES

Ros Asquith

as Letty Chubb

CORGI BOOKS

'Slaving breadwinners now come in two sexes,
but there's still no alternative for
the children' – L. Chubb

Contents

Bed-I-had-when-I-was-seven
Miniscule Room
Matchbox Cottage
Kewforloo
Sibling by Puke
Shoe-on-Stair
Nuclear Family Wasteland
Uvverfokesox
ME 2 NOT U

Dear Teenage Worrier(s),

Does your family make you as crazy as a gerbil on tequila? Is your home that one where the phone doesn't work

a) because the company cut it off?

2) because yr big brutha's playing Pluke Nukem with a spotti-nerd in Patagonia on it? or

3) because it's superglued to yr mum's ear?

Is it that one with a lukewarm bath (always occupied by some other family member or else their horrible old flannels), a dead hairdrier and a melting fridge that only contains cans of Old Bestard lager and weird smells?

Do you watch harrowing TV documentaries about children from Tragick broken homes and think, 'Compared to my place, this is a Disney cartoon'? Do you long for FREEDOM? Or to be little again? Take heart! This handy pocket guide will steer you through the labyrinth of Family Values: Parents who are Over-protective. Parents who don't-care-are-never-there, sisters, brothers, distant

1

relatives who descend loomingly at festive seasons to remind you why you haven't seen them all year, and the constant nag, drone, hum and whirr that litters the average Teenage Worrier's home.

However packed with glume and rage home life can be, however, it is usually better than living on newspapers in a shop doorway and I intend to demonstrate (ahem) how best to make the Teenage family years bearable for all of Yoooooooooooo, dearest fans, I mean readers. And hope that you may learn to embrace yr cold unwelcoming homes, with their darkened doors, both parents (if lucky enough to have same) out in bitter werld struggling to make ends meet instead of caring for only offspring Etck.

SO, whether you have no blood relatives at all, came out-of-a-test-tube and want to go back, are in Care, live in a mansion or a cardboard box, are an only child or the youngest of a family of twenty — I hope there are some tips and hints to keep you smiling through your pain until, arrrrg, you are grown-up and have to face ye dread responsibilities of creating your own little nest instead.

Let me know if I have left out any searing Family-Worries so that I can add them to my next volume . . .

Lurve,

Letty Chubb

And now . . . before I begin, a brief guide to my own beloved family . . .

Mother

Forty-something, always complaining about the menopause. This is not having a pause from men, as so many women wd like, but is about when your periods start to stop and, having complained about them for years, barmy mothers start to *miss* them, mourn for lost yoof and have parties for their last tampon Etck. At least this is one Worry I can cross off my list. Phew. My only mother is still raging at my father for never making any money and I have some sympathy with her, cos she was brought up V. Rich and it must be hard to be downwardly mobile when all the gurlz at the posh skule she went to have married bank managers, werld leaders Etck, or else become same themselves. Which, since she is supposed to be a feminist, I think she shld have done. All she does is work part-time in a children's library – moaning about falling literacy standards – and pretend to paint, moaning about sacrificing her Art for her family. I don't know who this Art is, but judging by the sprouts like meteorites and unfrozen mince she gives us, he's well out of it . . .

Unconscious Poetry in ye

Father

To earn his pittance while slaving over his 'novel',
my briefly successful dad spends most of his time
tinkering with old machinery and taking up floors
(see **Benjy**, below). He writes about Do-It-Yourself
and, as my Only Mother frequently remarks, whilst
toiling upstairs with a bucket: 'If you live with a
plumber, your loo never flushes.' Nothing in our
house works, even the front door. Things hang off
hinges, totter at precarious angles, have gaping
holes . . . Sometimes I am surprised to find the stairs
do actually lead to the top floor. One day, my father
is bound to take them down to 'see how they work'.
The only advantage in this for *moi*, is that he is
completely uninterested in how *I* work and therefore
does not nag me daily as some V. Caring dads seem
to do. Unless, of course, I want to do anything
remotely interesting like go to the chip shop after
dark. Then it's, how far away is it? Who are you
going with? Who'll be there? (A few old trouts
absorbed in their newspapers). When will you get
back? Etck Etck. Arg.

Brother One – Ashley, 19

All of you who have written to see if handsome,
witty, caring, tall Ashley has broken up with his
fiancée can hold yr breath. There is a ray of hope, as
she has asked for a 'cooling off' period. Gasp. Ashley

is therefore currently buried under a pile of seething hopeful gurlz for whom he Does Not Care, as he has eyes only for Caroline (as do my parents, as her folks are stinking rich and they foresee one less mouth to feed Etck). Otherwise, he is going to be a doctor, save the werld Etck. And, having been my frend for years, has V. Little time for *moi*.

Brother Two – Benjy: six going on forty-five, going on two

Aaaaaaaaah. Bless. Spherical Benjy. Juggle the letters, take away a single 'l' and you have Seraphic Benjy. He may look like a cherub, but he has temper of demented hyena and strength of Hercules.

When he isn't using me as a punch-bag, trampoline, or victim of practical jokes (like offering drink from Coke bottle he's filled with mixture of marmite, washing-up liquid, sprout water, TCP and lawn food), he is climbing into my bed each night because my Only Parents are snoring too loud to hear him. It is then that I feel V. Sorry for Benjy and we both feel that Nobody Cares together.

His fear of floors, sadly, is not abating despite my father's efforts to change lino in kitchen, carpet in bedroom, mat in bathroom Etck, to suit him. Only good thing is our house is so full of junk that floors are barely visible and it is possible to skip from Lego to teddy to pile of newspapers to pile of old socks Etck and barely touch floor for years.

7

Granny Chubb

My dad's mum, poorer than church ant, worked
fingers to bone as cleaner and now survives on half a
tin of cat food every other Friday. Prob my favourite
person in werld, as always has big hug, loads of
time, dry biscuit and warm friendly listening face
Etck.

Granny Gosling

My mother's mother. Was V. V. V. Rich (which is
how Ashley got posh public schooling) but has hit
Hard Times. Old habits die hard though and she
still can't understand why Mr Patel at the local cash-
and-carry won't deliver champagne, truffles Etck on
credit.

Pets

Are fleas pets? ↗

Rover
My old faithful cat of
cats, best pal in werld
and only member of
family that truly Cares
(I think). She makes me
sneeze and wheeze and
is covered with fleas,
gets stuck up trees, but
is always pleased when

she's on my knees, that's enough eeee's please
(wonder if I could be a poet, instead of a film
director?).

Horace
Benjy's horrible gerbil – shreds paper and goes
round and round all day on wheel, just like my
Adored Father thinks people who have to work in
offices do.

Kitty
Benjy's horrible kitten wot looks sweet, has teeth
like piranha and claws like tiger and wees
everywhere.

NB Chubb family has the usual assortment of aunts,
hangers-on Etck who emerge from lairs at Christmas
to be surprised how you've grown a few inches, how
spoilt you are, how they never had computer games
in their day but made do with a handful of dried
string Etck.

And now, on with my luxurious guide to
Surviving the Family . . . and remember, dear reader,
that I still have failed to conquer my superstition
about saying that werd about dying that rhymes
with 'breath'. I always use 'banana' instead.

Absence

Although supposed to make Heart Grow Fonder, absence can be taken Too Far, viz: foul, unthinking parents who are out every night asking poor Teenage Worrier to babysit. Worse still is when a parent goes off altogether, saying it is better for you than hearing them fight all yr life. (What they mean is, it is better for *them* to go, because then Flossie L'Amour will stop moaning about being Just a Plaything Etck). See also DIVORCE.

Adoption

It is V. Common fantasy of Teenage Worriers to think they are adopted and, instead of being only beloved offspring of Mr and Mrs Vole, 42 Humble Gardens, Cheapside, are in fact long-lost daughter of Syd Kool, rock star, or Daphne, Princess of Zaire, Etck. Although this is V. hurtful to your only parents, if you are not adopted, it is fun to dreeeam – and why not?

In Life as it actually lived, adoption is more tricky. If you are adopted, you are bound at some stage, to wonder why your only mum gave you away to a stranger. This can lead to serious pining and feelings of being Unloved for Yourself. The reasons, however, are often V. Good and V. Complicated. Many gurlz in the past were more or less forced to give up their babies at gunpoint rather than to disgrace their families Etck and, although things are better now, there are still many people who think, if a pregnancy is unwanted, it is better to have the baby adopted than to have an abortion.

Take comfort in the fact that adopted children are usually more Lurved and wanted than the rest of us, since your Adopting Parents were so V. Desperate for a Baby they went through all that paperwork, getting references to say they were not mass murderers Etck, and even agreed to take a baby as ugly, noisy Etck as yr good self. They shld get a medal.

Hopefully, you lurve your parents and think of them (rightly) as your 'real' parents. But there will always be a nagging Worry. What was my birth mother like? What happened? Etck. As you probably know, when you are eighteen (or seventeen, in Scotland) you are allowed to find out all this stuff and if you're really sure you want to, you can try to contact your birth parents. You may, however, find that when you *do* trace your 'real' mum to her palace, or hovel, that she is V. Embarrassed or furious to see you. She may have a family of seven who she's never told, Etck Etck. NEVER JUST TURN UP. Ring or write first. And take loads of advice from adoption agency Etck.

Go on Mum, admit it, I know I'm adopted - I can TAKE it..
But you're NOT darling. I PROMISE
POP!
was it something I said?

Armchairs

The purpose of the armchair as a family member is to give all the warmth, support and comfort that your overworked uncaring parents, carers Etck do not provide.

First, it is Always There in the Same Place when you return from school.

It never minds if you want to sit on its lap.

It is softer and cuddlier than the average adult.

It never tells you off or fights back, even if you punch it.

It stays in the same place, never wandering off to the shed saying don't bother me now.

It is also more likely to find things you have lost! And to give you money! Last time I looked under our armchair cushions I found 76p in old coins (sadly, four of them had chewing-gum so firmly stuck to them that even Adored Mother's nail file wouldn't get it off).

The only V. Sad thing about armchairs is that there are never enough of them and that everyone always wants the same one. Thus, tragickly, like all other things you Lurve in life, they cause rows, arguments, glume Etck.

Aunts

My Only Mother is always groaning that aunts have
it easy: they can come and pat their nieces and
nephews on the head, take them out for nice trips,
sweeties Etck and then swan off into distance
without ever cooking meal, washing socks Etck.
This is why lots of Teenage Worriers with childless
aunts think their aunties are lots more fun than their
poor old mums. But there are also V. Boring aunts
who only ever ask you about school as if that were
the most interesting thing in yr deprived and
anxious Existence, and how you are doing in your
exams Etck. Eeeeeek. These are the aunties who
never noticed inflation, cost of living index Etck,
and think you shld roll over waving yr feet in the air
like joyous puppy if they give you 50p.

Babies

There are two kinds of babies. One looks like a small
hairless rat, all pointy and wrinkly, the other looks
like a cross between Winston Churchill, and Sir
Elton John. Either kind are thought to be V.
Adorable and the height of fizzical purfection Etck
by their adoring mothers. BEWARE . . . this cld
happen to you! Most Teenage Worriers with babies
in the family, though, get them because their dad

has gone off with a younger model and decided to be a better parent to his new ickle baba than he ever was to the old ones, viz YOU. Breathe deeply and try to enjoy it. V. Hard. More of this later (See STEP-PARENTS).

A new baby in the family however, is not that rare. A curious nostalgia for those sounds and smells often afflicts women of thirty-something, or even

Love is Blind dept.

forty-something, and before you know it, bang goes the computer game, trainers Etck you were expecting as there is another mouth to feed, bootees by the hearth, nappies in the bin, bottles in the fridge, crying in the night Etck, Etck.

Moi self, I was nearly ten when ickle Benjy was born, and I remember it well . . . The Baby bukes all said: feed baby when he wants it, and soon he shld be in a four-hour feeding pattern. A newborn will sleep about 20 hours out of 24. Huh! Benjy fed every ten minutes and slept about half an hour a day . . .

But however tiresome and drooling a baby can be, they do have a built in 'love me' factor that overrides some of the selfish yearnings even of a Teenage Worrier. Don't get one of your own until you've passed the Teenage Years though, cos you'll never be a Teenager again and they are a V. V. Big responsibility, millstone round neck Etck if they are your very own.

Birthdays

In our house, birthdays come in five different packages:

My Mother, who never tires of telling the story of how my Adored Father forgot her thirtieth birthday until he Heard her mournful little voice humming 'Happy Birthday to Me'. He was so overwhelmed with guilt about this little oversight that he has been making it up to her ever since by reminding us when her birthday is about six months before it happens. He has even been known to buy her flowers. Whatever I get her, she never notices it half as much as Benjy's cards, which he always sticks bits of old spaghetti to and writes on them: *i LuV yoo MuM, hopy birdy*, using a different colour for each letter. At the sight of this grisly edible object each year my Only Mother (who is, after all, supposed to be an *artist*) swoons and exclaims upon his massive talent. At least it's the only time she doesn't correct his spelling . . .

My Father, who always says people don't know how lucky they are. He and Granny Chubb used to sit huddled around a cheerfully crackling matchstick, taking nips from the remains of a bottle of cooking sherry she found in the neighbours' bin, while he eagerly opened his lovingly-wrapped birthday parcel containing a single sock. And glad of it.

Ashley, who opens all his presents in about five seconds, kisses everybody in about a second-and-a-half, says it's his best birthday ever and goes out of the house saying Sharon Grone round the corner has promised him something a bit special. My dad always says to bring it back we'll all have a look at it, which usually leads to an argument.

Benjy, who got up at about two in the morning on his last birthday and crashed around the house, jumping over bare patches of floor and rattling cupboard doors. He became convinced his special present was hidden in Horace's cage so he let Horace out to investigate and then trod on him in the dark, concluding to his horror that the floor had turned into warm, squeaking wriggly stuff, and yelling so that lights went on all down the street. Adored Mother now plans to give Benjy two spoonfuls of Kalpol at bedtime before his next birthday, but it will just mean he will get up at three instead of two and fall downstairs.

Rover gets up on her birthday, stretches, rips up carpet, sofa Etck, hisses at Granny Chubb's slippers, slops milk on floor, has choking fit trying to eat Fatto Catto too fast, walks haughtily past hopeful looking brand-new toy mouse with ribbon tied round tail donated by El Chubb, and goes back to sleep. Rover's birthdays do not stand out like pyramids of Fatto Catto in her calendar I feel.

Did I say five? Of course, there is also the humble birthday of moi, but that, dear reader, is just like yr own. A long slow yearning, a fever of anticipation, a slow deflation (sounds V. like sex might be) as exciting parcel turns out to be puce and mustard bolero, wrong CD, Improving Buke, Etck. There is always a card from relative saying get yrself something lovely, with paperclip (but no money) attached, *no* card from true lurve Etck. And there is

18

An embroidery Kit!
My cup runneth over!

Embroider your Cushions

always a note of sadness in among the pleasure. No bloom without gloom, sez El Chubb. On each birthday, I always find one small bit of it goes slowly, spent yearning for my lost yoof, for when days were long and full of play, when parties were just about playing pass the parcel and being sick into your best frend's jelly. Now parties are a hive of seething Worries about who's snogging who? Who's wearing what? Who's there, who's not . . .

z z z Z Z z z z

Rover does not bother about parties

BROTHERS

My readers will know I have two of these items: a
Saint and a Nutcase. Living up to one (impossible)
and down to the other occupies great swathes of El
Chubb's psyche and most gurlz with brothers will
have similar probs to mine:

Brothers: get bigger helpings, even when they're
smaller.

Brothers: are often covered from head to foot in
mud but no-one seems to mind.

Brothers: play lots of shooting games, even in
houses that don't buy toy guns.

Brothers: need their confidence building up,
because boyz are falling behind gurlz . . . er, when I
luke at Big World, I see no sign of Women running
it.

Brothers: have Obsessions: football, computer
games, Lego, floors . . .

Brothers: are allowed to stay up later, go out more,
play music louder, not tidy up, never wash up, often
don't wash at all.

So much for the march of feminism. When I
moan to my Only Mother about her principles of
Equality she goes V. red and says she can't be
bothered to nag them all day. Why can she be
bothered to nag *me* all day then?

NB Teenage Worriers with sisters have same probs, joyz Etck as far as I can see, except they borrow yr clothes more. See SISTERS.

CARE

There is a Thingy yr life can be ruined by now – it is a dysfunctional family. The newspapers are full of it, viz: the Royal family is dysfunctional, Etck. But what it means to children in a really dysfunctional family in real Life, not palaces and nannies Etck, is that they are Put Into Care. The contradiction in putting kids 'In Care' is that it often means the exact opposite: social workers take them away from violent bullying drunk abusive parent and put them into Children's Homes where they are at risk of being abused, bullied Etck by complete strangers instead. Not surprisingly, most children prefer the Devil-they-know. But despite all the horrible things that can happen to kids, there *are* decent people out there who are longing to foster or adopt. If your own parent or carer is cruel or abusive in any way, it is V. Important to discuss it with someone outside yr home. A teacher or yr doctor, or even a V. Close frend. Try V. hard to get help.

CHORES

old socks are everywhere →

Chore Tips

Despite own household being lost cause, here are a few ways for Normal Teenage Worriers to negotiate chore-nagging:

1) Make parent or carer a cup of tea now and then. Once-yearly is about enough for them to think you are a Caring, sharing person.
b) Stuff socks Etck in drawer once a month.
C) When cutting crusts off bread, put them in bin. Better still, put them out for little birdies.
4) Eat straight out of fridge, to avoid plate-washing.
e) Try to remember to close fridge door.
6) Cook family meal now and then. Again, once yearly is often enough. It is also often enough to listen to chorus of praise afterwards: eg: 'It's lovely when you cook, darling, but every surface is covered with what seems to be glue and fluff? Part of cooking is also cleaning up, sweetheart.' (Or words to that effect.)

YES! An elderly SOCK!

mould

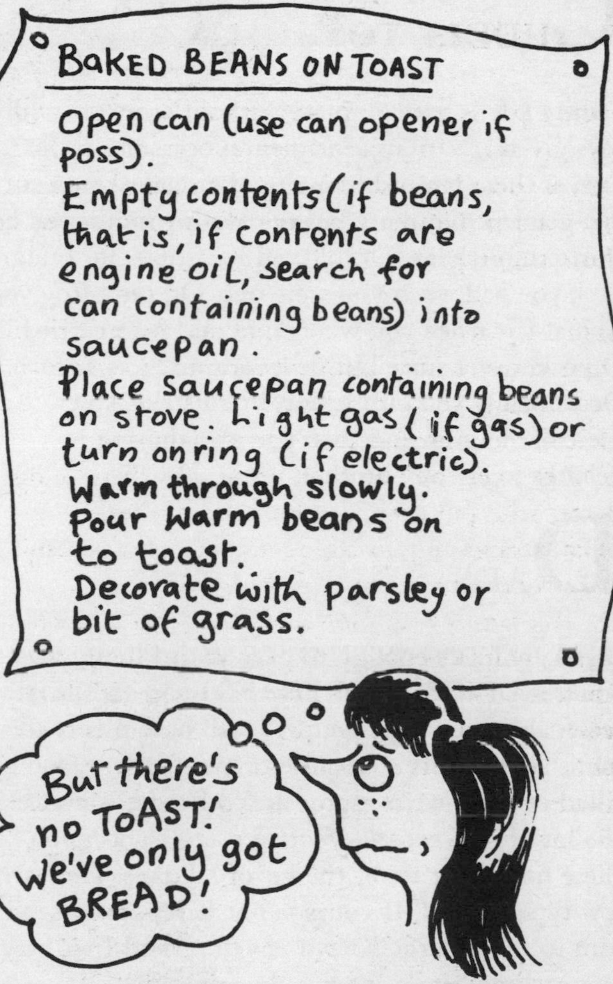

What DO they teach them at school dept?

Cuddly Toys

Family Life is not complete without army of cuddly toys given at various sentimental occasions so that each of them reminds you of sad or happy moment viz: giant penguin my father gave my mother on her thirtieth birthday. Or, old teddy, rabbit, fur budgie Etck you had when you were one. Or, puce frog you won at fair when you were eight and have carried in yr pocket ever since but never admitted to anyone. Occasionally you pull it out, by mistake, stuck to a piece of old gum and then you explain that it belongs to yr baby brother.

Dads

If you are lucky enough to have yr dad living with you (see DIVORCE, ORPHANS Etck) and he is reasonably kind Etck you will still have plenty to mone about. This is because to mone, grone, and be filled to brim with glume at Yuniverse is part of the lot of all Teenage Worriers and to occasion these noises is part of the lot of all dads. Here are a few types of dad. If yours is not here, please send him to me in large brown envelope and I will try and include him in next buke (yeeech).

Big Daddy

This is the V. Successful, striving, werld conquering Dad. He is V. Big at work, with thrusting car, wallet, Etck. When you were little you were V. Proud of him cos of all the V. Clever things he did. But you cld hardly remember  what he looked like, cos you were in bed when he got home and he left house before you woke up. Mr Big goes to lots of conferences at weekends, so you didn't see much of him then, either. You can remember at least four birthdays where he couldn't show up . . . (sound of violins, wail of bansheees Etck.)

Now you are a Teenage Worrier, he finds you much more interesting, inviting you to go with him to parties Etck. Sadly, you are not V. Keen on his frendz, life, werk. And he is V. V. V. not keen on all of yours. He has sent you to a posh skule, but wonders why he wasted the money since all you do is hang out with skinheads/hippies/rastas Etck. This kind of DAD is known as *work-rich*, *time-poor*.

Little Daddy

This is the kind of daddy
it can be hard to be
anything other than V.
Small with yrself. When

you were an ickle baba he seemed like a Big Daddy
because he was bigger than you, anyway. As you got
older you realized people often turned the lights out
and went out of the room while he was still in it,
gave him lots of V. Boring werk to do that he was
too nervous of The Sack to mone about (except at
home), pushed in front of him in kews, mistook him
for a twig, roll of lino, small wrinkly ornament
Etck. However, no-one lurves this kind of Daddy
like his own family, thank goodness, and lurve prob
keeps his world going round.

Bad Daddy

Drinks, chases women Not His Wife, drives too fast,
calls people he crashes into Blind, Morons Etck,
responds to complaints that He's Not Being Fair
with 'life's not fair', shouts, tells people criticizing
his bad habits Not To Give Him A Hard Time
Etck. Often had Bad Daddy himself. If you are
unlucky enough to have this kind of Daddy, you
may still be able to reach his Heart sometimes (most
people have one somewhere) but don't depend on it
lasting.

Let's <u>hope</u> this kind of DAD is going out of fashion...

Cross Daddy

Criticizes rather than shouts, doesn't drink (though it might help), thinks everything you do is a sign you're Not Trying. Like Bad Daddy, this type often had to deal with the same kind of stuff when they were little, and so are just passing it on. Trust yr own sense of what is Fair and what isn't. If yr daddy is cross because you haven't done something you promised to, or lied, or risked yr neck for something daft, think about saying Sorry. If yr Daddy is cross for no reason, it may be a one-off. If he's cross all the time fr nothing, enlist support from other members of yr family, and tell him you're a person too.

Dreaming Daddy

There is a DREAMER in Each one of us

Not a bad Daddy as they go, but it can get V. Annoying, espesh if you want to do most of the Dreaming around the house yrself. Dreaming Daddy is bored by the world of shopping lists, gerbil food, MOT tests, mixer-taps, dirty washing, moneing humanity, rubbish bags Etck, and who isn't? Shout in his ear once in a while to let him know you're still there.

Perfect Daddy

I know my own Adored Father isn't purrfect, but I
don't know any of my Frendz who've got a Perfect
Daddy either, at least to hear the way they talk
about it. Maybe they don't exist, but I can tell you
what my Perfect Daddy might be like:
1) V. Handsome and Witty, so all my Frendz think
he's Kule.
2) V. Decent and Honourable, so that he doesn't
reckon any of the people who think he's Handsome
and Witty wld be more Fun than his Adored
Spouse, Family Etck.
* 3) Rich. No explanation necessary. (see above)
4) Nobel Prizewinner. Virtue of this as (1), but also
for generating V. Proud feeling that he is helping to
Save Werld Etck. Also superior brane-power may be
in genes, rub off on offspring Etck.
5) Listening/Understanding – doesn't mind clothes
sodden with tears of Teenage Worriers, wails of
Nobody Cares Etck. When you're telling him How
You Feel, doesn't interrupt, or say I Felt The Same
At Yr Age, or paraphrase what you just said to mean
something Completely Different.

Mad Daddy

Can be quite closely related to Bad Daddy and Cross
Daddy, or suffer from delusions all the way from
believing the werld will discover their Genius one
day (which is qu. normal) to thinking they're
Napoleon and trying to direct the traffic in Slugg's

Lane to outflank the traffic in Ferret Cuttings
(which is not). Only if 1) it's behaviour that is
upsetting or hurting you, the family or anyone else,
or 2) you observe what seems to you V. Weird Stuff
going on over a long time and getting worse, shld
you Worry about it. The borderline between
eccentrick behaviour and madness is a narrow one
and sometimes only our Lurved Ones care about us
enough to know we're crossing it.

Divorce

Families need fathers, goes the old saying, as zillions
of single Mums trail to family support agencies Etck
attempting to get their offspring's dads to pay up
some dosh towards their bootees, nappeees, Etck. For
many of them it is tragick losing battle, so the Govt
is now keen for them to go out to work so their only
children see even less of them as well as not having a
dad around. Ho-hum. El Chubb sez: *Kidz need parents*!

And Teenage Worriers need them even more than
ickle babas, cos it's us lot that have to cope with
steaming mean streets full of drug-dealers Etck and
need cosy refuge, hot water bottle, listening ear Etck
which most parents are too busy to provide as it is. If
you have no parents you will certainly know what I
mean. So it is V. V. Hard, if you have been used to
having yr mum and dad around, to find that they
have actually chosen to separate.

Fact is, the nuclear family unit is a V. Rocky little boat, tossed on stormy seas, and vast amounts of tolerance are needed for ancient couple to stay together through thin and thick. But let's hear it for the kids! Did we ask to be born? Er, who knows? Probably we did. We were probably whirling about in space trying to get into heaven and being told, 'Go away, you've got to live 80 more lives yet before you're worthy of getting in on level one!' 'Oh, OK' we muttered, 'I'll go and find some Earthly parent then, and have another go.' And off we slouched, wings in pockets, kicking cosmic dust. Who knows?

I think it is always best to say how you REALLY FEEL. Of course, this will make them feel much more guilty even than your stiff upper lip Etck but at least it will:

a) possibly help them to come to some better arrangement (like seeing Flossie Scroggins every third Thursday, or only going out with Dominic L'Amour on Valentines Day)

b) or at least help them to respect your feelings and talk to you like an adult.

All this is V. Important, as Teenage Worriers spend a lot of time and energy on worrying how their parents are feeling and being V. Guilty cos their mother is in tears, on Prozac, or their father is drinking himself into an early banana Etck and they think it's their fault. Your parents' problems are NOT your fault. However V. Bad you think you might have been, you have NOT caused them to

31

separate (poss exception in case of Benjy, whose floor phobia does threaten family home).

If your parents already have divorced, you may well find compensations: eg: two homes to go to, lots more attention due to their guilt, V. kind step-parents Etck. All this, it must be said, can definitely be better than living with two adults who can't stand the sight of each other and are only staying together cos of you. And the biggest compensation of all, in a time of family breakdown, is knowing you are NOT ALONE.

Dummies

← wld like one of these moiself

If there's a baby in yr house, I V. Much hope there is also a dummy. They are V. Nice sucky things that give loads of comfort to ickle babas and also to their ickle mums who wld be going up wall otherwise at sound of baba yelling house down.

Embarrassment

Would adult dummies stop parents smoking?

Where to begin? As if the life of a Teenage Worrier wasn't embarrassing enough already, the Family rears its many bespectacled head to embarrass you at every opportunity. They SING, loudly, out-of-tune, V. Naff old songs at the supermarket check-out, just as you are languidly pretending to be shopping-alone, and eyeing-up Alfonso Dreamboat in the adjoining queue. They wear horrible scruffy clothes at parents' evenings and loudly boast about how they smoked 'a bit of dope themselves and it-didn't-do-them-any-harm' in front of yr head teacher!

Or V. Distant relatives wave the last picture of you they got, which was you naked, aged two, in a paddling pool IN FRONT of yr frendz . . .

Or they insist on phoning you at a party!

Or coming to pick you up from same cos it's after 8.30 p.m!

Or they make you wear a hat! Just cos there's a bit of snow!

Or buy you some grotty coat with a fur collar!

Or insist you wear gloves even if the only ones in the house have pink hippos on them!

Or, they knit you lime green and puce scarves . . . (I always slip on the one Granny Chubb knitted for me just as I go in her door, she can still make out the colours and it is a V. Small sacrifice to see her face light up with the joy of recognition).

34

FOSTERING

If there is serious trouble at home or yr folks are dead or in jail, you may well be fostered by some lurving person who makes jam sponges and is always home when you get back from skule. Foster-parents are checked out by local authorities Etck and, since they are actually offering to look after children rather than having to cope with result of burst condom Etck like so many 'real' parents, are often much better at it. Although there are bad foster-parents, the vast majority of them are V. Caring, and, if you become V. Happy with them, you may stay a long time, although fostering is usually temporary until you get back with your own flesh'n'bludde.

The family we all dream of, Noble Dad who earns fortune yet still has time to make moon rocket, buy designer trainers Etck and Noble Mum who earns fortune but is Always There For You exist only in fantasy. But if you've got just one adult who is a weeny bit like either of these, count blessings Etck (writhe, guilt, must practise what I preach Etck).

Am I V. Spoiled BRAT? Worry worry...

Garden

A garden is a place for ye familye to gather in Spring for egg-hunts, Summer for lazy barbecues, Autumn for bonfires, Winter for snowfights. Or so it goes in ye dreame family picture buke we all keep in our heads. This garden is big, with climbing frames, tree houses, pools Etck. True Life reveals few paradises such as these.

Grandparents

Tales at Granny's Knees.

In El Chubb's Dream Yuniverse, every Teenage Worrier wld be blessed with a full set of four grandparents and a couple of great grannies cackling in the corner, *comparing dentures*, and wittering on about how sweet the Teenage Worrier is, how well they remember their own Teenage years, how naughty they were themselves *holding hands without contraception, smoking behind bike shed* Etck, how they wld love to be young again but how nice it is to see young people enjoying themselves Etck and wouldn't they like a nice hot mug of cocoa Etck.

Real life, tragickally, sees that you are dead lucky if you've got one grandparent living and I realize I am V. Lucky to have two grannies (sadly, both grandpas popped their clogs before I was a twinkle in anyone's eye), and both are living in this country, but . . .

Granny Gosling is not a V. Perfect model. It is V. Difficult to think of anything to say to her, even in thank-you letters. If you don't write on the day you receive her present she will be on the phone to your aged anxious parent quick as a whippet to enquire if you have suffered Tragick Accident or if you are simply Ye Ungrateful Pigge Etck. If you *do* write, she will go as follows, viz: 'Goodness, Scarlett! You've discovered the application of the exclamation mark! But have you never encountered the comma, or the virtues of understatement?'

Granny Chubb, however, is model for all that is purrfect about human Nachure Etck. Poor but happy, she has the most valuable thing that anyone

37

can give a child, or a Teenage Worrier. And that is:
TIME. I know I can drop round to Granny Chubb's
sparkling hovel at any time of ye day or night and
she will be there with willing smile, stale dog
biscuit and freshly knitted bolero for *moi*. She is
clean and good and bright and honest as day is
long. I V. Much hope, that with her example
shining before me like bright starre, I will be able to
become like her too one day. And, *IT'S NOT FAIR*
that she can't afford one decent pair of specs when
Granny Gosling has three pairs.

Holidays

A time of joy and family bonding, when you can
cast off cares of werk and skule and splash happily in
ocean or laze by pule Etck, thinking happy thoughts
of lurve for each other and having V. Nice REST. If
yr family holiday doesn't sound quite like this, don't
despair. Most people get on worse on holiday than at
any other time of year. This is because all the
routine things that keep you going are stripped
away and you are confronted with: EACH OTHER.
Aargh, yeech, giveusabreak Etck.

Small
impression
of average
family holiday
WEATHER CONDITIONS

Home

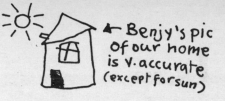

← Benjy's pic of our home is V. accurate (except for sun)

'*Home sweet home*'. '*Home is where the heart is*' '*There's no place like Home*'. It may be that cos we have all grown up with cute slogans like this lighting up in neon cross-stitch inside our brains, that our homes are usually so V. Disappointing. It is a big part of all yuman nachure to Dream and almost the whole part of a Teenage Worrier's nachure. But while ten-yr-old boyz and thrusting adults with bulging wallets Etck dream of mansions and parkland and helicopter pads, Teenage Worriers are looking for something more simple. This simple thing is called: *cosy*. Cosy could be a mat that says WELCOME. Cld be a real coal fire. Cld be just knowing there'll be a light on and something in the fridge. Being cosy is about feeling welcomed and comfy, feeling there's a big fat cushion to curl up on, a picture on the wall you have looked at all yr life, a couple of books in the bookcase that have always been there . . . If you are lucky enough to come Home to somewhere comfy and even luckier to find your mum or dad or other caring adult humming over a hot meal, you are lucky indeed. Sadly, many middle-aged worriers spoil this possible bliss by yelling 'Do your homework/oboe practice/thank-you letter' Etck the minute poor exhausted Teenage Worrier walks in the door.

INCEST

Do not confuse with incense. Incest is something
that smoulders all right, but not on a dish in the
corner, so don't go into the house of Abigail Knotte,
the hippy yoga teacher down the road and say 'what
a nice smell of incest'. Incest is sexual activity
between members of the same family, *but* unlike
when yr baby brother first hears about sex and asks
if he can try it with you, it is about akshul activity.
If anyone in yr family EVER touches you in a way
you don't like, or suggests something that is your
'little secret' that makes you feel creepy, get help
fast. They need help too, but you need it more.
When something like this happens, Boyz and Gurlz
often think they are the only person who it is
happening to, and they feel too scared to say
anything and suffer sometimes for years. Often they
can feel guilty, as though it's their fault, or they led
the adult on or even that they enjoyed it a bit. But it
is NOT their fault, ever, it is ALWAYS the adult's
fault and no adult shld ever ever make sexual
advances to a child. Neither shld a step-parent make
advances, even if you are sixteen. Yr home shld be a
place of safety from all this, so you HAVE to tell. If
there is no-one you trust enough to tell, ring
CHILDLINE (see numbers at end of buke) and they
will give you advice in confidence.

INDEPENDENCE

One of the V. Difficult things about being a
Teenage Worrier, is that you want to do everything,
all the time, be completely free of yr family, have no
guilt or responsibility, stay up till 2 a.m. dancing
every night Etck and, at exactly the SAME TIME,
you want to curl up in front of telly with hot choccy
watching yr Mum knit bedsocks. But how can you
prove to your parents that you can now tie own
shoelaces, catch bus, walk straight line (pref. not
under bus) Etck? Poor frantick parents are sure that
wild drugges are coursing through the veins of their
beloved offspring, and that old men in dirty
macintoshes are waiting to leap upon helpless Gurlz
beneath every broken street lamp.

So to convince yr parents you are going to be V.
Sensible, read a V. Good guide on drugs, tell your
folks you know all about them and exactly what to
do if you are offered any, recite Green Cross Code,
declare you will not go off in strangers' car Etck and
then put foot firmly out of door, telling frantick
elder when you will return. If you get back five mins
before the time you say for the first dozen times you
go out, frantik elder will breathe huge sigh of relief,
assume you are responsible (we hope) and then the
werld am your oyster. On V. Cold rainy nights when
all you want is aforesaid telly and hot choccy Etck

your old folks will prob start asking why don't you go out more? Haven't you got any frendz? Etck. So you can't win.

I T'S NOT FAIR NO, it's NOT (see QUARRELS)

Most common three words in English language. El Chubb's department of statistics show that these three werds are spoken 497 times more each day than those other three that you long to hear from lips of belurved Etck. Other close contenders are: 'I didn't do it' and 'It's not my fault'.

J OKES Ho Ho Ha Ha He He

Family jokes are Stuff of Life and V. good glue for sticking Members of Unit back together again after quarrels Etck. Being butt of family jokes is, however, not gratest fun in werld. 'Ho ho ho' chortle vast throng of relatives as you walk past, mystified, with 'Reduced to Clear' sign stuck on yr back. 'Sorry, Sharon's a bit tied up at the moment' sez hysterical older Brutha on phone to Greatest Lurve of Life as you struggle to untie yr shoe-laces from table-leg Etck.

Ha Ha Ho Ho Ha Ha Ho Ho Ha

April Fools jokes are other V. Jolly family things that V. Jolly family types love to chortle at, at yr expense. Benjy's favourite is to say Rover has been

Ha Ho Ho

run over. This is not my idea of fun. It doesn't matter that I check the calendar for months before April Fools' day. I still forget, every time. However, V. Easy to pay him back with practical joke, ie: bowl of custard by bedside so he steps straight in it on waking. Sadly, if I do such a thing, I suffer for days. 'Scarlett!' (my mother using my full name is V. Big Warning Sign) 'How could you! Poor Benjy! You KNOW he's scared of floors! You're old enough to know better.' Etck. Etck. Yawn. So much for family fun.

V.Unkind April Foole joke
perpetrated on moi last year...

KITCHENS

YES! Those socks are BACK

← crumbs

My mother's dream kitchen is like those ones you get dragged round on school visits to olde stateley homes Etck. Huge, clanking with pots the size of dustbins hanging from the ceiling, and strange pulleys, pestles, epistles Etck, throbbing with cooks, chefs, under-butlers, housemaids all bobbing and blushing and saying 'yes m'am' – a haven that she only has to breeze into with the week's menu and a condescending smirk. As it is, she blames her inability to cook anything but over boiled sprouts on the pre-War gas cooker my Only Father inherited from Granny Chubb. This is not a V. Successful ploy since my Only Father's memories of his mum's home-cooking are wreathed in the aroma of fresh-baked apple pies, mountains of cloudy mashed potato fluffier than a flock of sheep Etck. Granny Chubb provided all this food for my father and his horde of siblings on the wages of a cleaner, so why can't my mother do better? Depending on my mood, I take whichever side suits *moi* best, ie: *Mother's side* (feminist line): If you don't like it, cook it yourself. *Father's side*: Who mends the plumbing, wiring, takes up floors Etck? You expect me to cook as well?

Ye Kitchen is a sanctuary in some homes: cosy country-style range, kettle on hob Etck, smiles on

44

faces of occupants conceived by top designers, gleaming American-style worktops, scrubbed pine tables, fresh bunch of flowers, blah. Ours is more like war zone from *Newsnight*: V. Small formica-topped table covered in cigarette burns and coffee rings, ancient sink with permanently dripping tap, stove as above, miniscule fridge with ice compartment big enough for half fishfinger, drawers that won't open until pulled right out so all cutlery (three pieces) clangs on floor. Fetid hygiene-free cupboards crammed with broken pans, fine layer of volcanic ash covering everything . . .

TIPS AND HINTS FOR SMOOTHLY FUNCTIONING TEENAGE WORRIER'S KITCHEN LIFE

marrows? or socks?

I know many of my readers will be blessed with fancy gadgets like microwaves, freezers, dishwashers, coffee makers Etck, but for those of you like me, for whom the 20th century seems to have passed your parents by, there are ways of making kitchen life relatively stress-free:

1) After meal, scrape remains off plate and into bin. Leave plate to soak in lukewarm water (use it hot, if it werks) to avoid burnt chicken nugget Etck becoming eternally fused to plate.

2) Always wipe surfaces after meal, espesh surfaces of Yrself. Your sleeve will do, if, as in our home, you can never find cleanish dish cloth.

3) If you can't be bothered to wash up, eat straight

out of fridge by a) inserting head into fridge (fine on Summer mornings) or b) taking handfuls of food from within, using fingers.

LOO PAPER

← DON'T let a PUPPY near YOURS

Keep a roll in yr room. It is the only way of ensuring you have some when you need it. As my mother is fond of saying: 'I'm always buying rolls of loo paper, but it just gets USED UP'. This is undeniable. If it were not being used up, one dreads to think what the outcome wld be, though one cld possibly charge admission to house for all those curious to savour the ambiance of Life In The Middle Ages During Ye Plague. What does she *expect* us to do with it? Admire its noble, rounded form?

LOVE

Benjy hit the nail right on the head recently when, while humming *All You Need is Love* (my dad is constantly amazed by how well Benjy's generation know Beatles songs) he stopped in the middle and said: 'Love isn't all you need, is it. You need houses and food and . . .' What he was saying is, you need money. Love *and* money. Which is why, dear reader, I am writing this book. To get dosh to make my poor parents relax from the treadmill of unpaid bills,

46

crazy schemes for selling off one room of the house Etck Etck.

One of the first tasks of the Teenage Think Tank shld be to think up new alternatives to the family. But, I must confess that your family are the only ones you can rely on to lurve you more or less whatever you do and even though they criticize you night and day, you know they will stand by you in the end. It may be that money can buy you out of lots of family responsibilities and that rich loveless households lead to white-collar crime that never gets found out whereas poor loveless families lead to jail, but still, you do need the lerve, more than the money.

Probably the best test of lurve is to say: If a ten-ton block of concrete were poised above my (*insert brother, sister, auntie or whoever in this space*), would I feel worried that it wld crush them or worried that it wouldn't? Hmmmm . . .

MEAL-TIMES

I have a fantasy breakfast. I've seen it on TV. It's where an all-American Mom with smile designed by Interior Decorating firm (see KITCHENS) says in a lilting, sing-song voice, 'Come on down kids, bagels and cream cheese!' Right on cue, down come the Perfect Family: Lucinda, 17, pink cheeked and blonde, Ricky, 12, a bundle of cheerful exuberance, with a cheeky baseball cap tilted back and a ready joke for all; and cute little Mary-Lou, seven, in a flowered pinafore and bunches. 'Oh wow, Mom! Bagels!' they happily cry, as tall, lean, smiling Pop in jeans saunters in, arms full of oranges the size of California and squeezes them oh so freshly into a jug the size of The Universe. The Perfect Family may follow up with flapjacks, waffles and maple syrup, fresh fruit salad of mango and guava, before moving in an orderly fashion to a Tonka Toy 4x4 the size of a tank for their leisurely mountain drive to school.

Breakfast in *our* house sees my mother, on the rare occasions she is up, mournfully burning toast, shaking empty cornflakes packets and demanding why no-one but her ever does any shopping. My Only Father, when in paternal mood, will often spend the precious ten minutes of breakfast family-time, cutting the crusts of Benjy's toast or trying to make him a dinosaur-shaped peanut butter sandwich. If you have ever tried cutting white sliced bread with a dinosaur-shaped pastry cutter, you will have realized that the trampoline type texture of same leads to langwidge unsuitable for a family buke or to the casualty dept. Father alternates this gentle, see-what-I'll-do-for-my-children mode with a droning rant along the lines that he walked ten miles to school and back with a handful of hot gravel Etck and we don't know how spoilt/lucky/selfish/self-centred/grasping/self-indulgent/greedy Etck we are. Greedy! Huh! I

Bagels! ♥
Maple Syrup...
PANCAKES!
Eggs $unnyside up!
Freshly Squeezed
Guava Juice

One flaked corn
Drop of 4-day old
Milk.
Burnt crumb of toast
(at least soot conceals mould)

hurtle out of house with only one flaked corn in my poor lonely stomach, the wails of Benjy ('Not well! Not feel like school! Gonna be sick!') in my ears and only the dread knowledge that my PE kit is still pursuing its dreary journey going round and round in washing machine and therefore will give me an excuse to miss PE, to comfort me. So much for quality breakfast-time.

As for Sunday Lunch, wot used to be family occasion round roast beef Etck, there is now only glumey fumes of burning pot noodle since half family is vegetarian, quarter are suffering assorted food phobias and rest are at pub. Dream teas are no longer either . . . El Chubb longs for thinly sliced cucumber sarnies and choccy biscuits on fine bone china Etck, when she returns from skule . . . (sob).

Mums ♡! ♡?

Like Dads, Mums come in many forms. They have to be pretty disgraceful for most Teenage Worriers not to care about them at all though, so if you are really horrible to yr mum, ask yrself, does she deserve this? Your conscience will be yr guide. Do you, though, deserve what *she* is doing to you? Ask HER that – and her conscience will be *her* guide. Saying 'I only want the best for you' Etck simply isn't gude enough. Of course she does. And so do you. One of most frequent choruses from mothers is:

'I only want you to be Happy'. How helpful is that? How do you get to be Happy anyway? And can you ever be happy enough for your mum?

Here are a few types. If your mum isn't here, please send her to me so I can include her in next buke.

Career Mummy
V. Successful, striving, world conquering Mum. Like Big Daddy, she is V. Big at werk, with thrusting car, wallet, mobile phern Etck, but unlike Big Daddy she usually finds Handover to Au Pair at crack of dawn and return to resentful, whingeing offspring minutes before Bedtime harder to handle.

Just the same, she had to go to lots of conferences at weekends when you were little, on trips to New York to clinch Deal of Ye Century Etck, so you didn't see much of her. You can remember at least four birthdays where she couldn't show up . . . (sound of violins, wail of banshees Etck.)

Now you are a Teenage Worrier, she finds you both more interesting and possibly unfair competition because you are a disconcerting reminder that she is not getting any younger. Unlike Big Daddy, she is less likely to invite you out with her, espesh if you are going through Luminous Waif phase.

Self-Pitying Mummy
This is the kind of mummy who is always saying everything is Her Fault and, in a way that makes everybody feel they've got an itch they can't scratch, seems to be suggesting it's Their Fault Too, for being happier than she is. Like Horace, she goes round and round on a wheel, and the wheel seems to keep getting smaller and her with it. She can't Take Her Mind Off Things At Home By Going Out And Doing A Little Job Because Who'd Have Her At Her Age? She Doesn't Know How To Do Anything/Her Back Hurts/There's Nowhere To Park/She can't Have A Fling because She's An Old Bag/Your Father's A Jerk But I Can't Hurt Him/Sex Destroys Women/She can't Join A Book Group Because The Hamster Needs Feeding in the Evenings Etck Etck.

However, no-one lurves this kind of Mummy like her own family, thank goodness, and Lurve probly keeps her wheel going round. If you detect any similarities with Little Daddy, it is not coincidental.

Naughty Mummy
Drinks.

This, sadly, is often the Main Prob with Naughty Mummy. She may also Watch Telly Too Much/Play Bingo/Do The Lottery/Run Amok With the Creditcard/Flirt Past The Embarrassment Threshold/Wear Clothes that make Madonna look like Mother Teresa. This kind of Naughty Mummy is Doing The Best She Can, and doesn't realize people see it differently.

Naughty Mum always did believe in a mix of
Breast and Bottle...

NB Naughty Mummy is often seen by Werld as Respectable citizen.

Nagging Mummy

Like Cross Daddy, is driven by Compulsion that nobody's ever trying, espesh their Own Offspring. But in Nagging Mummy case, frustrated rage and sarcasm assisted by Eyes-To-Heaven disbelief that she cld have brought into the world someone so Totally Stoopid, Inept and unaware of Glorious-Role-in-Life as Yrself.

Like Cross Daddy, this type often had to deal with all this from their own Parents when they were little, and are passing it on with interest, in every

54

sense of the Werd. However, as with Cross Daddy, there may be a point to all this – if yr mum does not usually go on like this, you may Yrself have provided Straw That Breaks Camel's Back by yr own slobbishness, forgetfulness, unawareness that yr Mum is Also A Person Quite Like You Etck. However, if Yr Mum constantly nags, she may be unhappy, and you may be able to help her figure out why. Nagging can begin with many things, from concern that a Lurved One is Blowing It, to concern that a Lurved One is Making It The Way You Wished You Had, or Not Being The Only Kind of Person It's Worth Being and you have to Listen Hard to work out which is which.

Vague Mummy

Lurves visits to Nat Gallery to marvel at True Art, may even be in Lurve with True Art but married to miserable, sloshed, slovenly Unreliable Bert.

Like Dreaming Daddy, a Prob if you want to monopolise the *Mooning About In Dream State* department. But Vague Mummies are also Lurveing, because they believe that Yumans Falling On Each Other In Helpless Amazement is what's really happening, and anything other that that is just going to go down the pan at the Final Judgement. Tend to like blokes with V. Long Curly Hair, a throwback to 19th century poets Etck, who strode about in woodlands Etck thanx to allowances from rich relatives. Heart in Right Place, however.

Mad Mummy

As with Dads, can be qu. closely related to related categories. May shout all the time, curl up in corners In Despair, drink. May be completely normal person Driven To Limit. May hear voices, feel driven to commit violent or self-destructive act, feel werthless Etck, in which case urgent help is necessary. If Yr Mum thinks she is Boadicea, who almost repulsed the Roman invaders singlehanded driving only a horse-drawn Nissan Micra with sharp bits on the wheels, this may be merely a self-affirming fantasy that will pass, or she may be Totally Barking. As with Mad Daddy, I wld say the key factors are whether you feel personally distressed and oppressed by her behaviour, or whether you come to the conclusion that even the most broadminded person you know would reckon she is hanging perilously over the edge of Normal Behaviour. Families can be bad judges of this, because they're all in it together and the decline can be unnoticeable. Talk to yr closest friends, or even yr teachers and doctor.

Perfect Mummy

As readers will know, I am not afraid to call *moi*self a feminist. I am a firm believer in ye equality of ye sexes, but when I compare my idea of the Perfect Mummy, with the Purrfect Daddy above, I find some telling differences. I feel this shld give rise to sober contemplation on nature of Yuniverse Etck, but is prob more to do with ye slowly shifting roles and expectations. Our mother's generation was not equal to our father's, in treatment, or in expectation. And we treat them differently too. How will it be for us and our kids? I cannot help wondering . . .

SO: a Perfect Mummy, *moi* thinks, cld be any one of the types I have listed here, just so long as she's *your* Mum. Perfect Mummy shld always be free for a hug, always be ready to listen, be as happy as poss with her Own Life so she can let you be as Happy as poss with yours. She shld give you advice when you ask for it, but try not to when you don't. This doesn't sound like a lot, but it seems like it is . . .

Music

Can be V. Exhausting in families cos once you get more than two people in a room you get more than one kind of music being demanded . . . Our 'living' room often resounds to Radio 3 (my mother, harking back to classical music of early childhood, which wafted across rolling lawns crammed with ponies, groom Etck), *Teddy Bears Picnic* (Benjy's plastic record-player he had when he was two, which he still carries wherever he goes), Blind Willy Lemon's trumpet (Ashley is big jazz fan) and the excellent taste of *moi*, Letty Chubb, with my up-to-the-minute-state-of-the-art-newer-than-new Chumbawamba. 'Turn it down!' shouts my Only Father, unable to concentrate on his Heavy Metal.

'Which one?' we innocently reply.

Some Teenage worriers mone and drone about how their horrible parents force them to practise their violins, oboes Etck. They do not know how lucky they are (sob). Tragickly, my own familye never made us do any of that, so my latent talent as grate musician will be for ever under wraps. And since music and all ye arts are V. Underfunded and nobody on National Curriculum cares, most of my frendz at Sluggs have never tinkled the ivories Etck. Campaign for FREE MUSIC LESSONS (V. Good for soul).

NANNIES

Work-rich and time-poor parents salve their consciences by spending hard-earned dosh on these to control their unruly offspring. As soon as offspring have sprung off to school, they exchange Nanny for au pair if lucky enough to have big enough house with spare room. My frend Hazel has had thousands of au pairs, only one or two of whom cld speak more than three werds of English, so she always found them V. UNCOSY. My mother has spent her life threatening to get nannies and au pairs for us, but she has never had the money, or the space.

Being a V. Paranoid and suspicious person, I always expect nannies to be like Bette Davis in those old horror movies where the nice smiling mummy figure turns out to be evil scheming ghoul Etck, but I think good nannies and au pairs may be a lot more fun than parents for some kids. They don't get so wound up about you and are V. Keen to watch telly, gossip with pals Etck instead of nagging you. Also they have V. cosy phrases like 'You're not the only pebble on the beach' Etck which put you in yr place without putting you DOWN . . .

NEIGHBOURS

If lucky enough to have nice neighbours, they are a boon for Teenage Worriers. They will let you in if you have forgotten yr key, feed yr cat if you have forgotten that too Etck. We drew the line at Mrs Snivel down the road, when she broke a whole lot of neighbour-type rules at once and used our phone to ring Australia for five hours. But all we did was decline use of our phone, which since it's usually cut off anyway was no big thing. We still let her have a thimbleful of milk now and again – and she does the same for us.

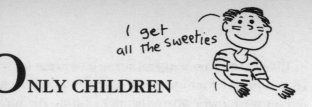
I get all the sweeties

ONLY CHILDREN

Only children are sometimes thought to be lonely
children. This is cos their parents usually feel V.
Guilty about them, trying to get them to have loads
of frendz they don't want Etck. In fact, only children
are V. Lucky in opinion of El Chubb, as they have
more space, clothes Etck, than the rest of us. They
also make V. Good frendz as they have more time to
give to their frendz, rather than having nagging
siblings demanding stuff from them. We are all
lonely islands spinning in space, after all, are we
not? Touched occasionally by the poetry in another
soul, only to be whisked again into the abyss
Etck . . .

ORPHANS

However much Yr Parents may Drive You Nutz, it's
hard to imagine life without them. Orphans have to
face up to this. The TV news is full of stories from
parts of the werld in which V. Cruel people are
creating this situation every day, and you try to
imagine what it must be like to be those children,
holding each others' hands or the hands of adults they
hardly know, and wondering what is going to happen
to them. In rare circumstances, because of accidents

or illness, this may happen also to children otherwise living much better lives. It prob goes to show that, rich or poor, being an orphan is V. Tough All Round.

We all need to feel loved, and parents, good ones and bad, are better at doing this than most of the alternatives. But, if you are lucky, there are also other Lurveing Members of Yr Family, and friends who know you and Lurve You. They can make it easier to do what seems hard at first – to look out at all the potentially wonderful things the world has to offer, and know that you can find other people to lurve, who will lurve you, too.

I think, perhaps, that if something V. Terrible happens to you like this, you can sometimes think that Lurve is no good because it can go away. Call me old-fashioned, Teenage Worriers, but I will never believe this, I hope.

OVER-PROTECTIVENESS

It may be a V. hard werld in which to bring up infant, junior and Teenage Worriers, but those poor kids like *moi* who were prevented from seeing '12' films until they were fourteen because it might frighten their little brothers or warp their minds Etck are at a distinct disadvantage in
   a) the playground.
   b) the cruel werld.

Parents

Parents, whether together, single, step, or divorced come in basic types:

Ideal
Tall, dashing father, miraculously wealthy and yet with endless time to spare for his offspring. He is the dad flying the kite on the heath, bouncing his toddler on his back-pack, offering to run your frendz

home when the last bus has gone Etck. Always checks where you're going in cheerful breezy free'n'easy way. Makes sure he knows who you're with, but never bangs on about who you shouldn't be with. Tells you all he can, helps you all he can, but never says *I told you so* . . . Is married to tall dashing mother, with ever-smiling rosy cheeks, neither glam nor frumpy, who loves her interesting yet not at all demanding work, and is always ready to drop it at an instant because she loves you so much more. These two run the ideal home, wafting with niffs of maple syrup, freshly squeezed oranges, crackling fires Etck. They do not exist on planet Earth, but then perhaps neither does the purrfect teenager . . .

TENSION ZONE

Demanding

These parents are always on your back: *Have you done homework/piano practice/emptied rubbish/tidied your room/ written your thank-you letters/rung your gran/gone to your tennis lesson? If so, why aren't you reading a book instead of watching the telly? Can't you think of anything useful to do with your time? Haven't you got a brain between your ears? You used to be so good at drawing/ballet/ needlework/ice skating, why have you stopped all that?* Or: *Why are you so interested in needlework/football/ reading? Why don't you hang out more with other kids your age?* Etck. Whatever you are doing, as far as these guys are concerned, it shld be something else. Or else you shld be doing it better, or more. This

type is summed up in scary werds of Hazel's dad:
She once told him: 'I'm doing my best', to which he
replied 'Your best isn't good enough.'

TIPS/HINTS: Always try to talk first, and explain
it makes you feel bad, glumey, a failure Etck, to be
nagged all time. Yr parent is V. Likely to love you,
or at least to think they do, so a small discussion
about love (see LOVE) might make them guilty. If
you really think it's impossible to please your folks,
it could be worth age-olde technique of
administering their own medicine. Ask why they
don't earn more, frinstance, or have as big a car as
the neighbours, or why they're not Prime Minister,
Hollywood director Etck. Make sure you do this in
sweet, honeyed tones of reason, not as long whinge.
They will, of course, go Nutz (sometimes followed
by chastened reason) but don't blame *moi* if this
backfires.

Teacher-types
Sometimes this type actually is a teacher in their
working life, but they don't have to be. They just
see it as their job to teach YOU. They are usually V.
sad not to have done more with their own lives, and
are V. keen to make every experience a 'learning
experience' for their lurved offspring, viz: you are
having nice quiet game of *Cluedo* and they lecture
you on complexities of legal system Etck.

HINTS: Own medicine technique. Tell yr parent
in earnest and minute detail, every single thing you

know about something V. dull and obscure (make sure it is the thing they will find least interesting in whole werld). You will find it V. boring learning all this and will have to pour over pages of dense medical tome, encyclopaedia Etck but it shld pay dividends.

Over-Protective

They will stop you crossing road alone until you
have yr own driving license and can prove you know
what a car indicator is. You see them anxiously
lurking about outside secondary schools wondering
if their child is hanging out with right types,
whether road surface is treacherous, streetlighting is
broken Etck. It is V. Nice to know they DO care,
but they need to know how much Worry they cause
their poor teenagers, viz: if poor teenager misses bus
she has visions of frantick mother dialling 999,
sueing bus company for negligence Etck. Also, if
you have been told to take care all yr life you are
bound to be V. Worried about what it is you are
supposed to take care OF. It is not a way to boost
confidence.

HINTS/TIPS: Point out lack of confidence above.
If this fails, just do the same to them. Insist on
knowing exactly what they are doing every second,
having all their phone numbers if they are at dinner.
Make sure your mum is always wrapped up in that
lovely beige, lumpy cardigan you bought her from
the charity shop, expecially for this purpose ('I know
it smells a bit, Mum, but it's really warm'). Only
allow her to take it off during month of August.

TAKE CARE

Mind the TRAFFIC

Be CAREFUL

DON'T talk to STRANGERS

We hear this allourlives. No wonder we're
Nervous wrecks...

Embarrassing

Usually the most embarrassing parents are the ones who try to be ever-young and your frend. They wear V. Short skirts (and that's just the Dads) and want to come to parties Etck with you. This must be nipped in bud V. Kwick. They play music V. Loud, sing in supermarkets, want to come to parties with you. Yeeech. Of course, if you have a V. V. Young single Mum who had you when she was fifteen, this cld be OK. But only just. She shld be living her life, not yours.

TIPS/HINTS: Tell Mum/Dad that you Like to be Alone sometimes . . .

Don't-Care, Never-There

Anyone worrying about over-protective parents might like to swop with the offspring of Don't-Care-Never-There types. One week and you'll be scuttling home to yr oppressive nest. Don't-Cares come in two distinct types: the V. V. Busy successful ones who are more interested in networking with their posh business or arty type pals than in the tortured agonies of Yr Sole . . .OR . . . slobbish types who sit in front of TV, computer, bottle of booze, deaf to any werld except that inside their own heads. They usually feel a Failure themselves, so are unlikely to give any Lurve or confidence to You.

TIPS/HINTS: Try telling them how you feel. See if you can come to some sort of deal, like: having

Do I HAVE to smoke, Dad? YUK

one evening when you actually talk to each other.
They may respond.

Over-Permissive

Teenage Worriers who love to complain about their
unkind parents who won't let them snort coke,
dance all night, have wild orgies Etck might like to
swap places with offspring of this lot. Nothing cld
be werse than V. over-permissive parents who set
NO BOUNDARIES. If there are NO
BOUNDARIES and yr parents let you do
everything, how can you be a whingeing rebel? Of
course, just like the animals in *Animal Farm*, it is
possible for Teenagers to do what they like,
whatever their folks say. Short of a ball and chain,
how can they stop you? But what some parents don't
know is that it can be fun being stopped. You want
an excuse not to go out doing scary, painful,
damaging things (as well as being allowed to do
lurvely, lush, naughty things). And these kinds of
parents are just too selfish to give it to you. They
love to boast about all the drugs they did themselves
centuries ago in the 70s before all their brain cells
died off, the wild times they had, how yr only young
once, it's your life, it's up to you Etck Etck. Closer
questioning of this type often reveals they only took
small hash cookie once and fainted, when they were
twenty-three. Remind them you are only 15 Etck
and too young to die.

69

Single

Now almost as common as married parents, so no need to feel you stick out like sore thumb and need years of V. Expensive therapy Etck to overcome trauma of:

a) Yr parents being unmarried.

b) Them being divorced.

c) Only ever knowing one of yr parents.

Life is pretty hard for single parents, as they have to earn a living, or fill in humiliating forms Etck to claim measly pittance, and they also have to provide all the love and food and washing Etck. If I were one, I know this wld make me have a shorter fuse and be more grumpy Etck, with my offspring. Unhappiness is what makes people bad-tempered, usually. If yr parent is V. Grumpy, why not ask them why they are so unhappy and why they are taking it out on you? This will make them think (we hope).

Pets

Pets, expecially cats (Rover might be reading this) can be V. Good Company for Teenage Worriers, because they Share Yr Pain with long, deep soulful looks. The cats in the Chubb household are chalk and cheese. Rover is Old, flea-bitten, ratty, demanding and adorable. Kitty is V. Cute to look at and everyone goes *aaaaaaaaah* but she spits and

scratches and wees on yr lap. I am V. Sick of
everyone paying more attention to Kitty and
neglecting Rover, faithful companion of my
childhood Etck. I will never abandon her despite
fact that I sneeze forty-five times each morning
before I even put foot out of bed cos she insists on
sharing my pillow.

Phone

V. Big source of quarrels as someone always on it
when you want it.

In El Chubb's dream dwelling, every Teenage
Worrier has their own private direct telephone line
or mobile, subsidised by the Govt to encourage you
to be a Consumer in Later Telephone Life. How else
are we to communicate in Soulless Yooniverse? One
V. Good thing about Over-protective parents is that
they are starting to get their kiddies mobile phones.
Heh! Heh! Sadly, these come complete with mobile

phone bills, so you are only allowed to use them in emergencies anyway. I am currently too scared to have one in case I get mugged for it, but I spect they'll soon be cheaper than packet of fruit gums to encourage users, and therefore of less interest to muggers than the laces of Yr Trainers.

QUARRELS SLAM! ARG! BANG! C·R·A·S·H

Just as it's a baby's job to cry, it's a family's job to fight. This does not make crying or fighting any more enjoyable for the people who have to listen to it, which is why you shld respect

a) yr neighbours and

b) yr family as far as is yumanly possible, by KEEPING THE VOLUME DOWN.

NB All fights are founded on one basic principle, although they take many different and subtle (and not-so-subtle) forms. This principle can be summed up in ye famous werds that echo through every cheery household, from high-rise flat to lowly cottage throughout ye lande. They are the three simple werds: *IT'S NOT FAIR*.

Let's run through one or two of Delia Chubbe's fighting recipes to see how these harmless-sounding werds emerge . . .

Usual start: one family member gets computer, sports top, dosh, that other family member wld V.

72

Badly like. Cries of: *IT'S NOT FAIR* ensue, with particular whingeing drawly note on last bit of 'fair', so werd goes high up into aaaaiiiir. Many of you nasty Teenage Worriers with younger siblings will leer at reading this page and rush to shove it in their face. However, take heed: it is no fun being youngest cos nothing is EVER fair. Older kids get to stay up longer, go out more, get more stuff of all kinds. Only answer is, 'Your turn will come.'

Now and then, *IT'S NOT FAIR* will be whined by older sibling. This is because being oldest is never fair either: you get to do homework, chores, Nobody Cares, while younger one gets all the cuddles, soft toys, cries of 'He's only little' Etck Etck. What is V. Not fair about being oldest, is, you are supposed to know better, and not cry *IT'S NOT FAIR*. You are supposed to be Grown-up, take it on chin Etck. The kind of examples our elders show us as spread over tabloids every day show none of them learnt how to button their lip and behave either. BUT, dearest reader, that does not mean we can't try.

One thing Teenage Worriers have got to learn: Life *Isn't* Fair. *IT'S NOT FAIR* that you live near nice skule and boy down road can't get in. *IT'S NOT FAIR* that you have a roof over yr head and gurl in cardboard box doesn't even have lid. If you want to get even more guilty (I lurve a bit of guilt . . . heh, heh, writhe), then try this one: *IT'S NOT FAIR* that you've got clean drinking water and electricity and

← Four
occupants

IT'S NOT FAIR

← Eight
occupants

← Ten
occupants

IT'S NOT FAIR

← Twelve
occupants

IT'S NOT FAIR

vast portions of werld are dying for lack of same . . .

The mission of El Chubb is to make Life as fair as poss. Wld only Fair thing be to issue each child with regulation dosh, clothes, sweeties Etck at exactly the same time? Or wld this make life V. DULL AND UNREWARDING?

Rooms

Tragickally, many of us spoilt middle-class teenage worriers were brought up with dolls' houses which contained vast numbers of rumes in which we could exercise our imaginations re wild wallpaper Etck. Real Life is different. I only know one actual house which has the *Cluedo*-style stuff of separate kitchen, dining room and drawing room. And even that house is short of a ballroom and library.

Rule one: however big your home is, one of your caring adults will always say: 'If only we had another room'. This imaginary room is for a study, or a spare bedroom. If they have any cash to slosh around, adults like to slosh it on completely ludicrous events like conservatories or kitchen extensions instead of buying their needy children interesting items like designer trainers, sports tops, game consoles Etck. The latter are too expensive, although a fractional price of the former. Weird.

Rule two: if money tight, then home improvements are effected by member of household.

In our case this means living without any walls or floors for months and sometimes years at a time. Worst of these is half-painted rooms.

ROYAL FAMILY

It is essential in the view of radical El Chubb that we retain ye royal family. They provide deep lessons for ye nation for, despite having all the rooms they cld want, plus ponies, videos, dosh Etck, they do not seem to be completely happy . . .

SISTERS

It is a V. Big tragedy for El Chubb that she has no sisters. I dream of lying in bed at night gossiping in Jane Austen style to my blood relations and soulmates about all the young soldiers, vicars, bums Etck that we might be getting off with. How we wld giggle and scheme! Sigh . . .

STEP-PARENTS

However bad thingz get between Adored Parents, I find it hard to imagine one of them being Somebody Else. However, I know from my Frendz that this not only happens, but can be purrfectly OK if the right people are involved. Nice people are nice people everywhere, and if they're nice to you and seem To Care, you usually respond in the end, even if they're replacing one of the people you thought would be part of yr homelife for ever, and thought they never could be Nice because they got off with Yr Mum/Dad and Broke Yr Werld In Two.

This is prob the TRUE meaning of 'step parent'.

TRADITION

Family traditions can range from V. Eccentric (like always calling yr Father 'Batface' or dancing on urban wasteland wearing nothing but wode on Midsummers Day) to V. Traditional, like having to

observe high-days and holidays that have gone back
generations, eg: fasting at Ramadan, never cutting
hair if you're a boy Sikh, knowing you'll shave it all
off one day if you're a gurl Hassidic Jew, Etck Etck.
Whatever our culture, it is V. Good to try to
understand its roots and reasons Etck, and not
assume something else is better just cos it seems
easier, or more fun at the time. White Western
culture is often attacked for being rootless and
without true vision (of God, Spiritual life, Etck) so if
you come from a family that does have a sense of
such things, you might just be better off than those
of us floating around clutching at straws Etck for
the Big Meaning. Of course, there are many
meanings, and we all, eventually, have to find our
own. Traditions can be useful for showing a path
either to go down, or as you get to think more about
the werld, to reject. Either way, traditions can be V.
Comforting and we all need them. And all families,
of all kinds, need . . .

TREATS

My mother has touching faith in outings as a time
for Family-bonding but I must admit I cannot
remember any of them happening without an
argument, viz: last time we went to zoo I was in V.
Animal Rights mode and V. grumpy about living
conditions, cages, Etck.

Only one way, in humble opinion of El Chubb, to make family outings a time of happiness, harmony Etck. And that's to allow everybody to choose their fave destination and all go separately since otherwise you will never agree. Sadly, this V. Unfair on Benjy-type younger sibling who's not yet able to cross road alone Etck and therefore has to tag along to the *Wonderful World of Butterflies* whether he likes it or not. Sensible tomes will recommend each member gets to choose one outing and everyone goes on it. In our family this wld mean five outings a year which is pushing ye finances somewhat as we are lucky if we get to go to a theme park once a decade.

T_V

Centuries ago when my mother was growing up, adults used to whinge on about how TV wld ruin children's eyesight, lives, brains Etck. Now it is V. difficult for many Teenage Worriers to prise their afflicted parents away from the box themselves, where they insist on watching game shows for middle-aged worriers instead of Important Searing documentaries or V. Important music and comedy shows. TVs in every room is only answer, though I gather that owing to V. Bad Artistick decline in telly programmes, fewer people are actually watching...

U_{NCLES}

Mysterious types who loom at Christmas, hopefully waving a tenner.

NB There are Teenage Worriers who have lots of uncles which is sometimes a name for their naughty mothers' boyfrendz. This also applies to flocks of 'aunties', ahem.

'Unusual'

Although families have always been a grate melting pot of V. Different types of people, you cld still be forgiven for thinking you are 'unusual' if your folks are from different cultures, mixed race, disabled, V. Old, gay, Etck Etck. So let's take these one by one:

We must make ALLOWANCES for Herbert. He's from a very UNUSUAL background...

?

...Ten generations of blond, blue eyed six footers

Poor lad

Different cultures

There are V. V. Few people who are British in the sense that every single one of their ancestors was born and bred here. We are all African if you look back to first human beings. Even so, we live in a racist culture and different groups of people have different beliefs and customs, so sometimes, however much you know it is silly, you may find it hard to 'fit in'. If you come from a V. traditional Asian or Jewish background frinstance, you may feel it is V. Unfair that other kids have more freedom than you. This is particularly true if, say, yr folks came here when you were a baby and have golden memories of their homeland, where gurlz behaved V. Nicely, so they think. The homeland's changed too, as an Indian mate of mine found when she went to visit there (dressed in a sari) and found all the other gurlz in jeans! Staying in touch with yr roots and culture is V. Important, though, and you have to get yr parents to understand the balance as much as poss.

Mixed Race

If one of yr folks is 'black' and the other 'white' (or, as L. Chubb prefers to call it, 'brown' or 'beige') then you may feel you don't fit in. Course you do. We are all different tones of beige, in fact, from dark to light. We are also (see above) all mixed race, so if anyone gets at you, just tell them we're all Africans at heart. Also,

All These Teenage Women are MIXED RACE

diversity means strength. One of the reasons incest is taboo is that in-breeding causes weakness, so the more different kinds of people who went into making the One-and-Only You, the better.

Disabled

If yr folks can't see, or hear, or walk, you will have a V. Different experience from most of us, and so will they. Often kids from parents with disabilities are much more adventurous and independent than most, cos they have had to be eyes and ears and legs for someone else. You prob feel V. Proud of yr folks, but if you are having a hard time or having to do too much, you cld contact a carers' organisation. This also goes for anyone whose parents are ill.

Gay

Since lots of people are gay, lots of gay people are bound to end up as parents. And they will be just as good, or just as bad, at it as anyone else. They cld feel under more pressure though, and so cld you, as the werld is cruel and kids are V. conservative. Try to forget all that rubbish in the tabloids about lesbian mums and gay dads which is about as stupid as the chants you used to get in the infants playground – remember, whichever boat you are in, there is always someone else in the same boat, and there are lots of organizations nowadays who you can ring up and go to talk to if you feel that you have no-one to share yr worries with.

V. Old

By the time you are a Teenage Worrier, yr parents will seem V. Old even if they had you when they were fifteen. Parents just seem to blur into each other. Now mums seem to be having babies at 60, you can bet there's always someone with a parent older than yours, anyway. The real root of fear about having older parents is that they might die. It is sad but true that we all face banana sometime, but since the average age for this is creeping up all the time, it is unlikely yr folks will pop off before you are an adult, even if they had you at 60, so try to put this Worry on the back-burner.

VICTIMS

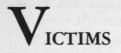

Who is the whinger in your family? There is always one who carries the merry family game of *It's Not Fair* to gargantuan dimensions, so that they are NEVER happy, but always moaning and droning on about what a V. Hard lot Mother Nature, the werld and werst of all, their ungrateful family has loaded them down with.

Real victims, though, who are being sexually mentally or physically abused, often don't whinge or even complain at all. This makes me feel V. Guilty when I think of it. There is apparently a syndrome in some abusive families where all the kids are treated fine except one. There was one case I read of where the youngest child was actually kept in a chicken coop, while everyone else was beautifully looked after. These are scary stories, but if you know anyone who is being terribly treated like this, or if you are yourself, it is V. Important to get help. Do not suffer in silence!!!!!!!!!!

VIOLENCE ← See numbers at end of buke

Much is written in ye tabloid newspapers about footballers and TV stars who beat up their wives. If this is going on in yr house, you really shld get help. Less is written about mental violence, which is harder to prove. You can be beaten up emotionally and psychologically, but there are no bruises to show the police. If either of yr folks is alcoholic, frinstance, this is V. Likely to be going on. Just because they aren't actually hitting you, doesn't mean they aren't hurting you. There are places to ring for children of alcoholics or other verbally or mentally abusive parents.

WEDDINGS 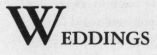 BOING-G-G

My Only Father refuses to attend weddings on principle as V. Borgwoise, decadent occasions for people to overspend, make promises they can't keep Etck . . . I have related my horrible experience at being bridesmaid in other tomes, but the general horror of family weddings still lurks over *moi*. I can't face thought of finding right clothes, suitable grimace on mug for hours Etck. I will not attend wedding again. Obvious exception for own, to Daniel . . . and wld also go if my parents ever bothered to get married. Huh.

X<small>MAS</small>

Have to say I V. Much hate this spelling for V. Nice werd 'Christmas', but couldn't think what else to put under 'X' and am firm and dewy-eyed believer in all celebrations. So whatever religion you are, each family has its own version of a feast day. Substitute your own favourite one here. For *moi*, Christmas is a time for ye family to come together in love and peace, ponder ye true meaning of life, sing carols round noble tree Etck. Much has been written about materialism, decline of True Spiritual meanings of season Etck, but El Chubb thinks that Teenage Worriers are ye grate supporters of Christmas. It is the one day you can avoid being nagged about homework as yr parent is too busy burning turkey Etck.

Y<small>ELLING</small>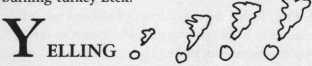

Yelling is a V. Good way of proving that the same sound is experienced differently by different people.

Let us take, frinstance, a normal Yell of, say, ten decibels as recorded by the El Chubb Impartiality Recording Mechanism. Let's say it is the yell of a normal mother at her normal daughter. This same yell will be heard at twenty zillion decibels by daughter, but her mother will hear it as a reasonable request in a moderate, if firm, voice.

Now let us take the purrfectly normal yell of a daughter at her mother (Impertinence at eighty zillion decibels as heard by mother, but a reasonable refusal as heard by daughter).

This startling insight can be used on many occasions and if it is the only pearl of wisdom in this little tome, then it is werth the cover price, is it not, dear fellow Worriers? If only we could learn to put ourselves in the place of others and see werld through their eyes. Sigh.

ZOOS

Aha! You thought the Zoo was somewhere you went to watch the cuddly python and to lament Humanity's relationship to grate Animal Kingdom, didn't you? But, no. The family is a zoo, and each member an animal. Have fun deciding which member of your family is which animal. A lickle cuddly squirrel? (Rats with nice tails, says my horrible father). A busy buzzing bee? (No chance in this house). A Noble Lion (Ashley, sigh). Your view of the animal

kingdom and yr family may well change as you
progress . . . according to the Chinese calendar I
think I was born in the year of the Rat, frinstance –
must check, cos rats are actually V. Intelligent and
caring but have, um, different aims than humanity's.

Have unpleasant feeling that I wld look
like THIS if transformed into animal.
Or THIS

✳

Wonder if I have probs with Inner Self?

ENDPIECE

And now, dear reader, we end our brief survey of the
Family, with all its many trials, tribulations, ups,
downs, joys, woes (get on with it – Ed), marred only by
the sinking feeling that I have but skimmed the tip of the
iceberg and hardly scratched the surface of all the many
variations of glume that may beset you in struggling with
yr family. Cruel truth is, that although each family is
different, we are all in same boat when it comes to choice:
you can choose your frendz, you may even be lucky enough
to choose yr work, or where to live, when you grow up, but
you have to make the best of whatever you've got,
familywise, until you leave home. So, unless they are cruel,
try to be kind to your poor old family. Nobody's purrfect,
not even you.

And we ask ourselves, does the purrfect Family exist?

My answer, dearest reader, is yes, briefly, for little
moments. These are worth treasuring in yr soul Etck. You
might like to use them in dim distant future when creating
yr own family.

Who knows? You might make a better job of it . . .

Yrs truly (heading for convent and life of quiet
contemplation in order to avoid V. Difficult task of
compromising high ideals and getting on with real people
like relatives)

Letty Chubb

Help!

Useful addresses/telephone numbers

Childline
Freephone 0800 1111
A confidential free 24 hour phone line for children in trouble or danger.

'Who Cares?' Trust
020 7251 3117
Run by and for young people in care, aiming to make life better for them.

Youth Access
020 8772 9900
Details of young people's counsellors throughout the country.

Adoption/tracing your birth parents
Essential to have counselling before attempting this.
At 18 (17 in Scotland) you can obtain your original birth certificate and sign a contact register by writing for an application form to:

The General Register Office, Smedley Hydro, Trafalgar Road, Birkdale, Southport, Merseyside PB8 2HH

Cruse Bereavement Care
0808 808 1677
Helpline for young people who have recently suffered the bereavement of a family member

The information above was correct at the time of going to press. If any errors or omissions occur, Random House Children's Books will be pleased to rectify at the earliest opportunity.

THE TEENAGE WORRIER'S POCKET GUIDE TO MIND & BODY

Ros Asquith

as Letty Chubb

CORGI BOOKS

Contents

Bluebird of HAPPINESS

Every silver lining has a CLOUD

Centres of Worry

Brow (OM)

Throat (HAM)

Heart (YAM)
see YOGA at end of buke for explanation

CURDS WHEY

THE VAST BUKE of CALM Vol XVIIII

Little Flower

Little dog stuff

Little roots

BIRDS don't get depressed

Really?

Letty Chubb, glorying in Nachure and at One with Universe

Feather Bed
Om Sweet Om
Doors-of-Perception
Chakraton
Serendipity-on-Sea
Attitudesville
Nr Futon
Lake of Sagacity
Mount Rapport
Genderfree
IM OK UR OK

Dear Teenage Worrier(s),

Well, hey, wow, chill out, yo dude, respeck. Sitting here on my mountain retreat and gazing down at all you lowly mortals from my dazzling new platitude, I mean altitude, I see how mere specks we are in ye grate Universe; how all our Worries, taken in ye grate context of Eternity, are but tiny morsels to ye Gods of Life. And how, if we can but throw off the sheckles (shouldn't that be shackles? — Ed) *of psychic glume, we can fly with the bumblebee and sing with the sparrow.*

Now don't go getting the idea that moi, El Chubb, has entirely changed her character by indulging in some Magickal new technique of meditation, or suddenly discovered I have grate healing Powers, or gone off to Tibet in arms of lissom guru to say 'Zen' — or is it 'Om' — no, but I have, amid the festering glume of LIFE-threatening

1

WORRY, found a shaft of joy occasionally in dabbling in the hinterland of alternative therapies Etck. It seems to *moi* that anything, however small, that one can do to stave off the abyss that otherwise threatens the yoof of the planet is worth a try. And, dear reader, when you are Worry-free, you can dispense your calm, your inner joy, your oneness with Yooniverse Etck to other, humbler, needier souls than yrself. Thus the journey I am encouraging you to embark on will be not just a selfish one, but one guaranteed to bring light and peace to help alleviate the sufferings of others (grone, pass sick bag, that's enuf do-gooding – Ed).

Seriously, if you can feel happier yourself, then those around you will also benefit. Wish my own parents wld try some of these remedies to ease the pain of the yuman condition instead of drowning their higher feelings in old-fashioned escapes of booze, fags and V. Bad Temper, though must admit their heart-rending hippified attempts at Meditation, Yoga Etck were not V. Grate success, as I reveal below. Trouble with older generation is they just give up so kwick. I think they suffer from Attention Deficit Disorder.

I believe, if Teenage Worriers cld set V. Good example and practise ancient arts of relaxation Etck, we wld all find our Worries dissolving in sea of Bliss (also, get less cold sores, pustules Etck). However, this humble buke is not a health guide, so don't pore over it hoping to get cures for athlete's foot Etck. It shld be used more as a spirichual awareness type thing.

Yours, dreamily progressing towards Higher Plane. Arg! Where's my hot water bottle? Lucky rabbit's foot? Teddy? (This may be harder than it looks),

Letty Chubb

And now . . . before I plunge headlong into my alphabet of CALM, a few measured werds about the reasons I need this buke (similar, hopefully, to the reasons you too will need it) . . .

Mind Worries

Although I wd like to tell you that writing five thousand bukes about Worry has calmed my seething soul Etck, I must admit to not having quite conquered the vast list of glumes, neuroses, habitz, anxieties, fears, phobias, nervous disorders Etck Etck that continue to plague *moi*.

Frinstance, I still use 'banana' instead of saying or writing the word about dying that rhymes with 'breath'. This makes my skule work V. Difficult, cos obviously I can't just put 'banana' in an essay, so I use all sorts of other methods to avoid using ye dreade word. I wd like to conquer this prob before I do GCSEs, as I often spend hours searching for alternatives which cld result in V. Blank exam papers. Also, sarcastic remarks from teachers about whether phrases like 'Hurtling into the chasm of doom' are suitable for life cycle of tadpole.

I still twist my fringe, stroke my lucky rabbit's foot in times of stress and also have compulsive desire to do small things twice. By small things, I mean, if I drop something, I touch the floor twice, or I turn a light on and off twice Etck. I also Worry about Tragick decline of kindness, future of planet, whether I will get a job, whether I will live to see tomorrow, whether my family will survive Etck Etck, yeech.

So this buke will hopefully be a self-help manual for *moi*, so that by the time I get to the end of it I will have . . . well . . . reached the end of it.

Body Worries

Moi →

Endless. Being lanky Etck. Round folks do not have any sympathy for *moi*, but I looooong to be cuddly. While I know this shows that no-one is ever satisfied and that it it V. Stooopid to whinge on about how you look and there are more important things in life Etck, I still say: just you try looking like a boot-lace with the strength of a flea Etck and see how YOU feel. Also, it is V. Hard for us gurlz who have NO bazooms, waiting for them to come. Also, I measure my nose, tape back my flapping ears, apply zappo to my spotz and zappex to my cold sores daily. Never mind the usual litany of hourly Worries, viz: PMT, brain tumours, nits, athlete's foot, varoukas, ultimately ending in banana Etck Etck. Hopefully, this little tome will enable readers to Worry less about outward appearances and concentrate more on the Inner Self.

A Little Note on the Family Worries that occupy my mind and surround my body

* **Father** locked in isolation with computer pretending to write novel but actually playing GOD (computer game where you build own Universe). Scratches measly living by writing Do-It-Yourself articles, which he practises at home to catastrophic effect.

* **Mother** who wants to be artist, but scuffs heels in kiddies section of local library, scorning state of modern edukashun and Worrying about her offspring.

* **Luny brother Benjy** (5), who is phobic about floors, has smile of angel and teeth of *Jaws*.

* **Perfect brother Ashley** (18), at Oxford (whinge, groan, class hatred Etck) learning to be brain surgeon Etck and fighting off swooning females.

* **V Nice granny Chubb**, now retired from cleaning other people's homes, so spends all day hoovering doilies and knitting boleros for *moi*.

* **V. old cat**, who I lurve, Rover (female).

ACNE

It is A Well Known Fact that other people not
Worrying about the things you Worry about can be
V. Worrying. However, there is one thing that all
Teenage Worriers agree on Worrying about and this
is Acne. (A V. V. tiny minority do not Worry about
this because they never get it, but I do not count
them as Teenage Worriers at all, or indeed members
of The Alleged Yuman Race of any description.)

I believe Acne is prufe that either God does not
exist, or that He or She went out for a long lunch
when the concept of Teenagers was being worked
on, and left it to a bunch of low-grade angels on a
Welfare to Work scheme. Acne is V. definitely an
ailment invented by somebody with a V. sick sense
of humour, possibly with extensive experience in
terrorist bomb-making factories. Set the time, then
guide Innocent Yoof right up to the gates of
Adulthood, cackle ye celestial delinquents,
rubbing their wings with unholy glee. Let them see
Ye Promised Land of Deep Voices, Gropings Behind
Bicycle Sheds, Cleavage, Mobile Phones, Driving A
Car, Summoning Waiters, Going Bankrupt with
Student Loans Etck, and then – *blip! splap! pflurrrp!
kerpoww!* – stand back and watch while a meteorite
shower of red blobs with pulsating white nuclei

7

THREE SUCCESSFUL CURES for ACNE

This Teenage Worrier used Chinese herbs...

This Teenage Worrier used TIME...

This Teenage Worrier used L. Chubb's patent ACNE-PACK. Send SAE for bag in four colourways: Beige, sand, pebble or stone. + cheque for £494.99 payable to L. Chubb PLC.

erupts from some dark region of Inner Space within Ye Luckless Teenage Worrier and lays waste to all exposed areas of previously unblemished skin. There are more than 50 types of acne apparently (yeech!), and of course Teenage Worriers suffering from it believe that they have all the variations at the same time.

Akshully, all is not lost. Acne vulgaris is the most common type – so named because a lot of people get it, not because it comes on once you start thinking about SEX. It starts in the sebaceous glands, which are there to put out fatty substances that stop your skin from looking like an old walnut, but which go ballistic when stimulated by all the hormones that start hammering around yr Bod during puberty. Most people get a version with little inflammation, or one with little inflamed pustules that don't leave scars unless you keep hacking at them with yr fingernails, and there are ointments to reduce the inflammation during the year or so (groan) the condition usually lasts. There is a more unpleasant version of acne which attacks the skin deeper down and can leave lasting scars, but V. few Teenage Worriers are unlucky enough to get this – and yr doc may then recommend more drastic measures, inc. ultraviolet light, antibiotics or even hormone treatment. But most cases of acne a) don't look half as bad to others as they do to you, and b) are just another thing you have in common with a large number of yr frendz, and c) go away sooner than you think. Try not to PICK or SQUEEEEEEZE too much though, because a) you might leave permanent marks, and b) yr mum will get fed up with bringing in teams of industrial cleaners to hose down the bathroom mirror.

Acupuncture

V. Ancient technique of Chinese medicine, now V. Popular in right-on muesli circles. It involves having needles stuck in you and works by stimulating energy flows in V. Mysterious pathways in the Bod, identified by mysterious Chinese doctors thousands of years ago  but not the same as the pathways of the Nervous, or Worrying, system. Acupuncture therefore has V. Exciting descriptions of things you might have wrong with you, viz: to whit, *Liver Fire* Etck, which sounds much more interesting than 'tummy upset' or something.

Acupuncture has been proven by suspicious Western scientists Etck to work V. Well on some conditions like certain skin problems, muscle strains

Etck. It doesn't hurt, and fans say it can give you V. Nice feeling of energy, clear head Etck, as well as fixing whatever your prob was. If you fancy it, try it once to see if you like it, but don't believe it can cure all ills or avoid going to a regular doctor for anything that might turn out to be serious.

NB Some people may have an AIDS Worry about infected needles Etck, but if you go to an Acupuncturist who's a member of an accepted practitioners' group you will have no probs because they will sterilize all needles V. Carefully and may even offer to use brand new disposable ones each time.

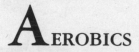EROBICS

See EXERCISE.

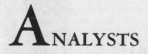NALYSTS

Unhappy People are V. good subjects for analysts, as they can find out lots of things that cause unhappiness (ie: Nasty teacher when you were five, nasty parents all the time, no potty training, too much potty training, absence or excess of soya milk Etck Etck) and therefore at least go on being Unhappy with Good Reasons. Happy people sometimes visit analysts too, to iron out some little problem and then realize how many V. V. Big Probs they could be suffering from without realizing it.

For many probs afflicting Teenage Worriers, a

listening ear from a kind and sympathetic person can be the V. best solution. So don't think that seeing a counsellor, analyst, therapist or any other professional means you've failed. Almost everyone needs someone like this at some point in their lives, many of us V. Often. I'm personally saving Deep Analysis for when I'm older and richer, but there is lots of help available to Teenage Worriers who are depressed or Worried. You only have to ask.

See also DEPRESSION.

Apple

According to ye Holy Christian Bible, temptation started here. Since Adam was involved I'm not surprised (phew, cold shower). But it turns out it was only a mouldy old apple. Myself, I was more affected by Snow White than Eve. I still can't eat a shiny red apple, just in case some mirror somewhere is saying 'I'm the Fairest of them All' . . . And some Evil Queen is lurking awaiting her chance to garrotte me. But maybe it wld also mean a Prince is lying in waiting, chance wld be a fine thing.

However, if you wish to be healthy in MIND and BODY, an apple a day will be V. useful (old sayings always best dept).

Ask yrself.
Is my LIFE more like this? ^   or this?

Banana

In case you think this buke is turning into fruit salad, this is just little reminder that Banana is the word I am forced, due to phobic terror, to use instead of the one about dying that rhymes with 'breath'. All Teenagers, and especially Teenage Worriers, will spend time Worrying about this subject. The Worries go something like this:

1 What if I die?
2 What if my parents die?
3 What if anyone else I truly love dies?
4 What is banana itself like?

The V. diff thing about this subject is that to be haunted by fear of banana is part of what makes us human. It is the one question to which there are both many answers and no answer. You may have strong religious beliefs, but you cannot know what it is like until you do it.

My own V. Humble contribution is the following V. Comforting thought, which goes like this:

There are two options: a) Either you die and nothing happens, in which case you don't know anything about it, OR: b) You die and something else happens, which is bound to be quite interesting.

The above inclines me to believe that one

14

shouldn't be fearful, but naturally it doesn't stop anyone Worrying about those they love and imagining how they cld possibly survive without them. Another thing Teenage Worriers do often is to feel responsible for the banana of someone they loved. Examples of this are like when you go out slamming door and saying you hate yr parents and never want to see them again and then that VERY SAME DAY both parents are devoured by white rhino, as in a Roald Dahl book. Or, you have a frend with fatal illness and think if you can sit by her bed every second and do nothing but think of her day and night and never go to loo Etck, she will somehow get better. And she dies while you are having a wee. Sorry to sound glib to any of you who have had experiences similar to these, but Teenage Worriers have a bad habit of blaming themselves. They think: *If I'd phoned her when I said, she wouldn't have taken that bus and then she wouldn't have walked down that street just at the moment that the Jumbo jet fell on her head.* OR: *If I had only got up earlier, I wouldn't have been late to meet him and he wld still be here now instead of under speeding milk-float* Etck.

This kind of Worry can certainly drive you mad, BUT these things are accidents and illnesses. They are NEVER *your* fault. If someone you love has died, *talk* to someone about how you feel. If frendz aren't enuf, try counselling.

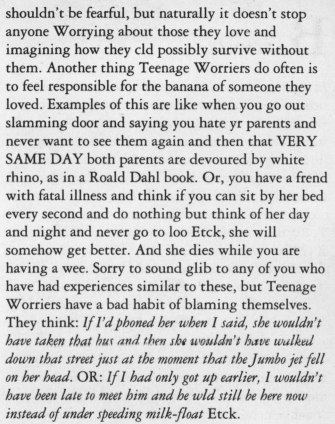

← Hope
springs
eternal

Bazooms

According to most Teenage Worriers, these are either too big (chance wld be fine thing, whinge, glume) or too small. In the case of many Teenage Worriers, they have not emerged at all. Yet others are buying vast unwearable cardigans in order to muzzle and disguise them. In this unwinnable situation, L. Chubb advises all Teenage Worriers to take deep breath (espesh in case of those of you with V. Big ones, har har) and meditate on vastness, not of yr Bitz, but of universe. Muse also on tininess (not of your bitz), but of atoms.

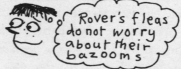

Rover's fleas do not worry about their bazooms

We are all titchy blobes whizzing in space, and whether our even titchier protuberances are big or small is not — is it? — a thing that shld take up much of our valuable brain space. This shld, but may not, stop you Worrying, but I am fed up with sexist rubbish about bazooms, and, contrary to all my other bukes on the subject, have promised self to throw away all those padded bras and learn to enjoy life without them — and sadly, this means without any bazooms either, since mine will obv not now ever come.

16

A few T-shirts from L. Chubb's Bazoom range.

Bermuda Triangle

A creeeeeepy area in the Atlantic Ocean off Florida where a number of ships and aircraft have vanished. Also known as the Devil's Triangle, and a source of V. Grate Worry to Teenage Worriers with Travel-Phobia (eg: 'Will I ever HAVE to go to, or through Bermuda?') who have watched too many XYZ FILES Etck. Worriers! Harken to El Chubb: So far, there has been no scientific evidence of any unusual Phenomena involved in the disappearances. So it's not creeeeeepy after all. Yippeeee. Or boo-hoo, depending on mood.

Cults

Arrgh, glume, POVERTY Etck.

Many unsuspecting idealistic Teenage Worriers have been attracted to cults – organizations that promise an End to War, or starvation or the discovery of a new sisterly love – only to find they are working 25 hours a day for a handful of hot gruel and sleeping on floors while some rich guru is spending their wages on Rolls Royces. If you are seeking spiritual awareness, it's better to go for one of really long-standing well-established religions.

See also RELIGION.

Deodorants

There are now so many anti-pong sprays for so many parts of the Body, that I wonder if SEX will soon come to an end, cos no-one will be aroused by erotic smell of opposite gender any more. Limit deodorants to under arms and just wash everything else V. nicely is L. Chubb's advice. Deodorants for naughty Bits can sting and also upset natural balance of fluids Etck.

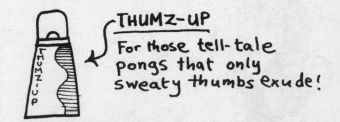

THUMZ-UP
For those tell-tale pongs that only sweaty thumbs exude!

Depression

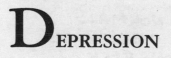

Granny Gosling says she doesn't believe in Depression. Even when they say on the weather reports that A Severe Depression Is Forming over the Atlantic, she thinks it's a sign that the Elements just ought to pull themselves together. But for just

Wooooooooooaooo
NOBODY understands the AGONY OF my SOUL

NB Above is V. NORMAL
result of: PMT, overtiredness,
lack of nice nosh Etck.
Do not confuse Teenage
Worrier's GLUME with
Depression.

about everybody else, Depression is real enough, and
most of us believe we've had at least one, and maybe
know somebody who has them so often it's a Major
Worry.

But Depression is not just being unhappy because
Leonardo di Yum Yum married somebody out of
Babewatch you could never get to look like even if
you ran yr own 24-hours-a-day team of plastic
surgeons, or because yr Gerbil doesn't go on its
wheel any more, or you think yr Bazooms have
akshully got smaller than last month. That is just
getting in a Bad Mood and happens to everybody,
particularly Teenage Worriers. It's not an illness,
because if something nice happens, you can snap out
of it, and that can be anything from a bright blue
sky, to getting free tickets for Green Spume's 900th
farewell concert at *The Hovel*. Even the way you feel
if something Really Awful happens to a Frend or
someone in yr Family, though it may make you feel
Terrible for ages, is not the same as Depression –
though it can turn into one, and sometimes you
need help to get you over a real shock or
bereavement.

A serious Depression goes deeper even than this,
and is harder to get rid of. When you are Depressed,
you have no energy, and nothing seems worth
doing. (According to Only Mother, Teenage
Worriers are all like this, but it is not a reliable
Medical Judgement.) A Depressed Person may feel
V. Slow and Sluggish, be unable to enjoy anything,

and sometimes unable to sleep (the latter is definitely a sign that Teenage Worriers As A Hole don't suffer from it). Or they may alternate between Slowness and hurtling around bouncing off People and Thingz like a pinball, which is called Manic-Depression.

Depression is the most common prob psychiatrists have to deal with, and it's been known about since the famous Greek GP, Hippocrates, who called it melancholia. Stresses of Life can bring it on, but so can not having enough of certain Vital Substances that make the brain work, particularly a chemical called serotonin. Doctors mainly treat depression with drugs (to restore whatever Brainstuff yr Bod isn't producing by itself) or psychotherapy (trying to find out what the real reason for Yr Misery is) and sometimes both together. Depression can be eased, and often cured completely, by the right treatment and it's V. silly to leave a serious depressive illness untreated.

D<small>IETS</small> ← Boo

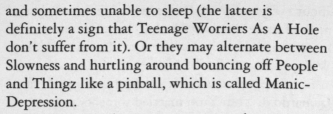

V. Large numbers of Teenage Worriers are worried about their Body weight and it is a V. grate shame that the media is so obsessed by the way people look that you just don't see images of ordinary faces any where. The *only* suitable diet for Teenage Worriers is a healthy one, including loads of lovely carbohydrates (bread and pasta and potatoes), loads of lovely vitamins and minerals (fruit and veg), loads of lovely protein (eggs and fish and meat and cheese and nuts and soya beans), loads of lovely variety like rice and pulses and everything yummy. And grate a little fudge on everything if poss.

If **no fudge**, choccy will do nicely. Slurp.

Dieting also usually doesn't work for a V. V. Simple reason (LISTEN TO THIS BIT AND SHOW IT TO YOUR MUM): When you lose weight, your Body sets off starvation alarm signals and your metabolism slows down. You lose some weight, but it is muscle and water, *not fat*. Meanwhile, your Body gets better at storing what fat it can because it is Worried it will starve otherwise – so that you actually get *fatter* when you *stop* dieting. This why 95%(ish) of dieters go back to their normal weight within a couple of years. This might sound SCARY, but it isn't – it's reassuring. Your hardworking little (or long or squishy or knobbly) Body is trying to look after you. It has your best interests at heart.

Now forget about food. Except to enjoy it when it's there. Yum, Slurp. More Bigger Fudge Now.

See also EATING DISORDERS.

DISABILITY

If you have a disability you will prob Worry more about everything in this buke than Teenage Worriers who don't. Physical disabilities are bound to make you feel you'll have trouble finding lurve Etck, and it's pretty infuriating to read about stupid Teenage Worriers who are Worrying about their bazooms, spotz Etck if you haven't got a working pair of legs – particularly if you are also spotty and bazoom-free.

I am always V. Surprised how incredibly patient and nice lots of disabled people are, given that I wld want to boot most able-bodied people in the bum if I was them, including *moi*self. Here I am, whingeing on about size of hooter, flappy ears, Etck, and I never stop to think what it wld be like if I couldn't see, or hear, or run. However, everything (even Worrying) is relative and the last thing you want or need if you have disabilities is to be pitied.

One V. Imp fact is to realize you are not ALONE. In fact, one in four people in the UK is either disabled or has a disabled person amongst their family or frendz. Plus, in 1995, there was an act passed by Parliament (The Disability Discrimination Act) which focused on rights for the disabled. Let's hope it starts working soon. So here are a few tips for able-bodied folk:

YES, ONE in FOUR

24

And how are **WE** today?

Me? Or my Wheels?

Speak to the person, not the wheelchair.

If someone can't see, always say yr own name and the name of the person you're speaking to, so they can follow the conversation.

Don't assume someone with a disability is ill, they're probably healthier than you.

Wise up and don't use horrible thoughtless insults like 'He's spastic' about anyone, disabled or not.

Offer assistance to a disabled Teenage Worrier if you want, but wait for them to accept. (Imagine being propelled over the road when you never wanted to cross it in the first place!)

If you have a disability, chances are you'll already have pals in a similar situation. If not, it's good to join a group so you can share mones and grones. CAMPAIGN for people with disabilities to have the same opportunities as everyone else. Good access for wheelchairs. Use of swimming pools, recreational facilities Etck. And, V. Important, ART. If El Chubb had to condense the most V. Important things to keep MIND and BODY together, they wld probably be the great Outdoors (ie: getting into countryside, or parks) and CREATIVITY (painting, drawing, writing, acting). These are things that will bring happiness to nearly everyone if they are allowed to do them and no-one laughs.

Dreams

There are many bukes and therapies that try to teach you how to remember yr dreams and understand them, one of the most charming of which is to get two pillows, sit on one and pretend the other is your dream. Then you talk to the dream pillow. Later, you sit on the dream pillow and become the dream talking back to you. This sounds sweet and I wld V. Much like to try it, but have sneaking feeling cushion wld turn into giant nightmare-filled beanbag and envelop *moi*.

Although I'm sure devoting whole life to study of dreams and their meaning in seething unconscious is V. Noble, I am personally more interested in Daydreams. I have V. Strong desire to put Daydreams on National Curriculum and make it a compulsory GCSE subject for all Teenage Worriers. Why? Cos allowing yrself time to daydream is V. Imp for the soothing of the Soul. Finding time just to let yr thoughts run free may be qu hard in small chaotic households where TV is always blaring, but I find the bath (scented with V. aromatic bubbles Etck) the best place on rare occasions when it is a) unoccupied, and b) hot.

See also MEDITATION.

DRINK

Here are a few boozy facts (hic):

Alcohol slows down the brain.

It affects gurlz quicker than boyz.

The lighter you are, the more quickly you're drunk.

One thousand under-15s are admitted to hospital every year with acute alcohol poisoning.

Alcohol is V. Fattening.

Enuf said. And anyway, just the sight of a shandy makes *moi* fall over waving spindly legs in air and singing *I Did It My Way*.

What is IN these pills?

DRUGS

Drugs, whether prescribed or not, do work. That is, they affect our delicate systems. We have little receptors all over us that respond to drugs – and one V. Recent theory is that MIND and BODY are so linked that the little information substances (hormones, endorphines, peptides) wander about the Body influencing our cells and therefore how we feel and behave. So our Body is full of natural drugs, and the more we can get them to work, the less we feel in need of other drugs, either for 'recreational' purposes, or even, possibly, for medicinal ones. Exercise, for instance, releases endorphines, which give a natural 'high' and so on.

Obviously, just as people vary in appearance, they also vary in their chemical make-up. Some seem low in serotonin, a neurotransmitter that affects mood (see DEPRESSION), and others low in one or other of the zillions of chemicals that zoom around our little frames. Not surprisingly, this leads many human beans, some of them Teenage Worriers, to seek solace in MIND-altering substances. BUT, argues El Chubb, the more we can tap into our own Inner resources and find all the useful little substances in our own bods, the less likely we are to feel the need for other stuff.

Also, as any true Teenage Worriers knows, there

What happened next day....

N.B. The Teenage Worrier on the right tragickly forgot to put on his trousers. Since he also forgot his boxer shorts (and never wears Y fronts) he was expelled... And all because of just one night in the embrace of Cruella de Drugge...

is no way of knowing what is in the tab of E or whatever you might be tempted by, so FEAR is a good reason to steer clear. I reckon they'll legalize cannabis (which loads of people smoke and believe does V. little harm) one of these days, which at least will mean father can't be retrospectively arrested, but fear of Breaking the Law and getting arrested, fined or even jailed is enuf for *moi* to steer clear. My real fear, though, is of going really MAD as a result of drugges, cos I have seen it happen.

Also, if you feel under pressure cos it seems everyone is doing it, take comfort from the fact that this just isn't true. Latest statistics in 14–16-yr-old age group show that 30% have tried illegal drugs. This means that 70% haven't! Also, many of the 30% will only have tried something once. More disconcertingly, by the age of 22, 90% of Teenage Worriers will have been offered illegal drugges. So learning to say 'no' is werth practising.

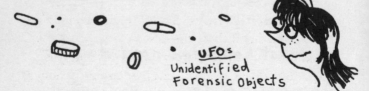

UFOs
Unidentified
Forensic Objects

NB Heroin now V. Easily available. Do not be persuaded that chasing dragon will turn you into Train-Spotting heroin(e), however. It will not only cost you arm and leg but V. Likely life – or else life-long misery of addiction.

Eating Disorders

Eating disorders like *anorexia*, where the sufferer starves themselves and believes they are fat even when they're painfully thin, and *bulimia*, where the sufferer alternately starves and binges, emptying the contents of the fridge into gob and then deliberately making themselves throw up, are on the increase. If you are genuinely overweight and also very tired, you could have a thyroid disorder and it is simple to check this with a blood test.

Warning signs to look out for **in Eating Disorders**:
* An obsession with food, but a reluctance to eat.
* Not liking to share meals with other people – and leaving the table early.
* Secretive behaviour.
* Frequent self weighing.
* And, obviously, loss of weight.

Although it sound as though these disorders are self-inflicted and therefore deserve no understanding, they are in fact *very dangerous* and it is important to get medical and psychological help as soon as possible. In so far as the reasons for them are known, they seem to do with being over-stressed and worried and trying to get control over just one thing in yr life.

See also SELF-HARM.

Erogenous Zones

Erogenous Zones are mainly supposed to be just the Naughty Bits . . . but for Teenage Worriers all zones are erogenous if fondled – or even sensuously skimmed – by the Right Person. I am V. Disappointed the Erogenous is not included among the Zones you can visit on a one-day Travelcard.

I think the Govt should declare a few square miles of each city to be an erogenous zone, where people can parade about canoodling Etck with no fear of harassment, wearing exactly what they like and doing nothing but ROMANTIC stuff. Cameras and professional hookers wld have to be excluded, as this would all be for free. Sigh.

Exercise

What middle-aged Worriers do to work off excesses of their yoof. Teenage Worriers shld be nicely toned anyway and I find walking into our apology of a sitting room and turning on the TV (if I can find it amid the piles of DIY magazines, Lego and tubes of oil paint left by my revolting family) quite enough exercise thank you V. Much. However, this is a responsible tome so I shld stress that exercise is V. Imp if you want to feel healthy in MIND and BODY.

If you get to like your bod and feed it nice nourishing stuff and exercise it, it will wag its tail at you. Fat dogs don't get enough exercise. How many people are mean enough not to exercise their dogs? But we're too mean to exercise ourselves, viz: be sure to walk upstairs rather than take a lift Etck (unless you are in the top floor of a tower block, in which case it wld be V. tiring) or in a house (in which case it wld be V. Unlikely you wld have a lift). Actually,

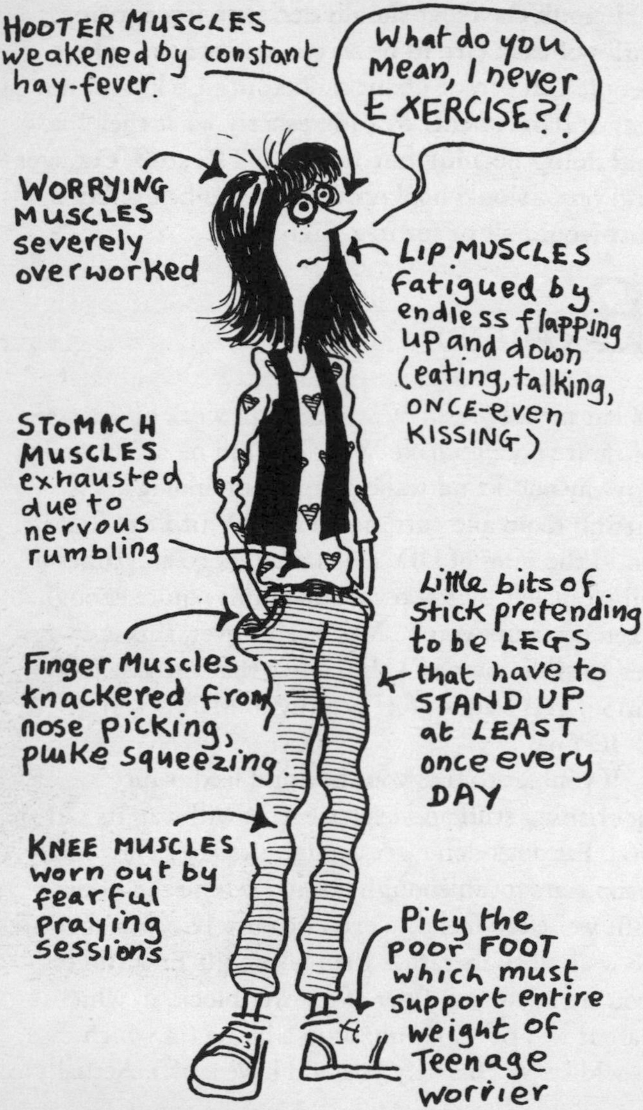

HOOTER MUSCLES weakened by constant hay-fever.
What do you Mean, I never EXERCISE?!
WORRYING MUSCLES severely overworked
LIP MUSCLES fatigued by endless flapping up and down (eating, talking, ONCE-even KISSING)
STOMACH MUSCLES exhausted due to nervous rumbling
Little bits of stick pretending to be LEGS that have to STAND UP at LEAST once every DAY
Finger Muscles knackered from nose picking, puke squeezing.
KNEE MUSCLES worn out by fearful praying sessions
Pity the poor FOOT which must support entire weight of Teenage worrier

I'm not sure when this advice is supposed to apply, so I will move on to next thing, which is:

EL CHUBB'S EXERCISE TIPS
Consider the following:
1) Walk to school if poss, swing arms in merry fashion. Sometimes, run.
b) If near river, row to school (rowing exercises all of you at once, and with V. Little effort).
3) Consider joining in organized stuff at school a bit more. Why not actually climb that rope instead of staring glumily at it as though it is a dinosaur neck from dume?
D) How about actually, er, joining in with OTHER people (Radical!). Table tennis is V. Good if you have just one frend, but if you have more than one, team games can be a larf.
e) Dance!
f) Yoga! (V. gentle, spirichual Etck.)
7) Wild Nookie (chance wld be fine thing).
8) Hide channel-changer and walk to TV set.

Exhausting toe exercise

Eyes

Windows to soul. Huh. If
this were true then I wd
be living with Adam
Stone in eternal bliss, cos
his eyes definitely said I
lurve you for ever and
then he bunked off to Los Angeles . . .

Fantasy

I have a big prob distinguishing between Fantasy
and Reality, partly because I spend much more of
my time doing the former than living in the latter. I
used to fantasize about winning the Grand National,
Horse of the Year Show Etck, then had V. Brief
period of knowing I wld be V. Famous model (ho
ho). Now I know I will become V. Werld-famous
Film Director (this will actually happen, so doesn't
count as Fantasy). But I waste hours inventing
scenarios about exactly what Adam and I will say to
each other when we are looking back on our loooong
happy relationship, and all over the Western Werld
there are Teenage Worriers fantasizing about what
they will say when Leonardo di Yum Yum turns his
dazzling orbs towards their Kate Winsome-style

tressess . . . sigh . . . and so it goes on . . . and on.

I suppose, once you are on the roller-coaster of Fantasy you never get off. Though I am sure that when my lurve is requited, I will be able to concentrate my LIFE energies on Film Directing and use my powers of Fantasy to help mankind with V. Moving Imaginative documentaries about Human Suffering Etck.

Feng shui

Hey, wow, you can tone up yr room! This ancient Chinese Art sez: make yr environment happy to make yr self happy. It sez that each area of the house you live in represents a different area of yr life – and then goes on to say scary things like, if your loo is in your wealth area then you're prob flushing all dosh down toilet. This is obviously true in Chubb household. NB Feng Shui cure for this is always keeping loo seat down. (I imagine they mean while yr not using it . . .)

Teenage Worriers are, of course, helpless victims of their parents when it comes to houses: ie: we have V. Little control over whether we live in neat tidy flat or tousled mansion, Etck. But you might try a little Feng Shui in yr own bedrume, involving mirrors, little silver balls, crystals, jolly plants Etck.

NB Tell yr folks that, according to Feng Shui, yr front door and hall are V. Imp. Make em as nice, light, clutter-free Etck as poss. Arg, brief survey of hall at current moment reveals:

On floor: Two pairs trainers, four other shoes (not matching), one Wellington boot, eighteen leaflets for pizzas, nine leaflets for double-glazing, sixteen circulars, three cards from postman asking parents to collect unpaid-for mail, Rover's toy mouse, nasty rotten green thing that may be ancient tangerine, four little plastic figures, two toy cars, a kite, a ping-pong bat, last year's Christmas *Beano*, a bicycle pump, lots of fluff (it's quite tidy just now).
On wall: Two hooks, astonishingly supporting fifteen garments that resemble jackets, five scarves, a broken umbrella and three baseball caps.

GARDENS

Getting back to soil where we all come from and to which we must one day return (sigh) is obviously a V. Deep and meaningful soulful experience for many.

I have been somewhat disappointed in gardening attempts, possibly due to small concrete yard, but I do not deny that the joy of seeing tiny shoot emerging, heralding Spring, changing seasons etck can be V. Rewarding and it is my ambition to get Granny Chubb a little patch of Earth one day in which to exercise her remarkable green fingers (even her fish fingers are green, ha ha yeeech).

Seed tended by Moi

Seed tended by
Granny Chubb

What she does with a window-box should be at the Chelsea Flower Show. *Moi* thinks spending some time growing things is V. Creative and good for soul, espesh if it's nice herbs to flavour the fish fingers Etck.

Glumes

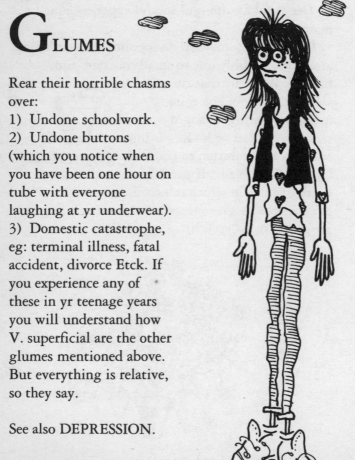

Rear their horrible chasms over:
1) Undone schoolwork.
2) Undone buttons (which you notice when you have been one hour on tube with everyone laughing at yr underwear).
3) Domestic catastrophe, eg: terminal illness, fatal accident, divorce Etck. If you experience any of these in yr teenage years you will understand how V. superficial are the other glumes mentioned above. But everything is relative, so they say.

See also DEPRESSION.

Habits

BURP Hic Right! Knowotimean?

People often don't tell
you about Yr Bad Habits
to be kind, but I think it
is a mark of a True Friend that they do. To judge by
Adored Parents, Granny Chubb Etck, habits that are
quite unnoticeable in Yoof can become V.
Maddening and Conspicuous as you get older and
care less and less what anybody thinks, so it wld be
good to try to zap them early on.

Habitz that tend to revolt others are: loud farting
followed by louder larfter (as though you think it V.
Clever to fart); overt nose-picking involving
examination of yr bogeys; saying 'Right' or 'D'You
know what I mean' after every three werds.

My own Habits include: obsession with even
numbers which leads to *moi* wanting to touch
everything twice; biting nails to kwick and therefore
never cultivating Cruella de Ville style talons;
twisting my fringe around my finger, which leads to
finger becoming V. Tangled in knots of wig;
carrying lucky rabbit's foot (animal-lovers note: not
real rabbit's foot) at all times; kissing pictures of my
family before I go to sleep; praying at all times in
unlikely situations.

The above all embarrass *moi*, but are not too
harmful to anyone else (I think).

41

H APPINESS

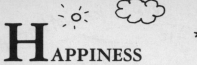

A V. Famous Person of Eng Lit (W. H. Auden, who
wrote the V. Sad poem in *Four Weddings and a
Funeral*) said that we have a Duty to Be Happy. This
seems to *moi* to be one of the more interesting
thingz that Persons of Eng Lit have said about how
we should all carry on.

The Happiest Person I Know is Granny Chubb.
She's kind to everybody, has fun doing V. Simple
things she's done for years, and doesn't yearn for
things she'll never have. I can't work out if this is
because the Game of Life has slowed down as far as
she's concerned, and she's just given up (having high
expectations of anything is, of course, a bit of waste
of time in our family anyway) or because she's
always been a Zen Buddhist disguised with a pac-a-
mac and a Tesco bag, and her Needs Are Few. I
think the real reason is that she's delighted with
anything that turns up to make her Happy, has been
putting on a Happy Vibe as a bit of a duty to those
around her for so long it became second nature, and
is open to Happiness but doesn't expect some
strange Elixir called Happiness out of Life as a
Right. She is a Model to *moi*, though maybe you can
only get to behave like that by being Old.

Granny Chubb

Hot Water Bottle

HOT CHOCCY

Rover, fleas and all

Yes! FUDGE!

V. Gude Buke by Ivan' Idear

Just a sprinkling of the AVAILABLE (as opposed to unavailable, sob.....) things that make MOI happy.....

Health

Ever had one of those weeks (months, years . . .) where everything seems to go wrong and you feel like doing nothing but groning soulfully under duvet or gazing tragickly at rain dripping down glumey window Etck? And THEN you get flu, complete with exploding head, throbbing eyelids, graveyard wheeze, suppurating hooter — and you realize that compared to this you have been feeling just great?

Just a small sample of supplies I like to carry if I'm away for more than a couple of hours.

It is at times like this that the av Teenage Worrier promises never to complain about anything ever again if they can only just feel well. Although this is usually a short-lived promise, it is werth remembering that good health is one of ye grate gifts of life and werth hanging on to at all costs.

HERBS

V. Ancient remedies for a
zillion ills can be found growing
in the gardens of our once grate
nation – but understanding them wld
take a herbal encyclopaedia. I am V. Fond
of herbs and spices on food Etck . . . so by all
means add a little rosemary and tarragon to yr
chips or fudge.

V. strange-but-true Fact that while Rosemary and
Basil are names for herbs *and* people, Tarragon and
Coriander are not. It is werthless but charming
thoughts such as these that provide much solace for
*moi*self.

HIPS

Sexiest bit of bod in Adam's case. Strong Sekshul
connotations generally, due to muscular
requirements involved in Doing It, Giving Birth
Etck. Hip movements in dancing Etck thus often
targeted by V. Bossy People in Olden Times (1950s)
as signs of moral decline in Teenagers. Must admit
however the El Chubb attempts at dirty dancing
look like stick insect suddenly discovering it has
taken up residence on bonfire.

Homeopathy

Our own noble Royal Family believes in
Homeopathy, which enables them to live to Great
Ages and thus have even more time for being
dysfunctional, shooting wildlife, shaking hands with
baffled passers-by Etck. Homeopathy is treating like
with like, which means giving you a bit of the
disease so you don't catch the full unedited version.
On this basis, Ickle Benjy is obviously a
Homeopathist, because when he gets a cold he blows
V. tiny missiles of snot out of his V. tiny nostrils at
moi, but it hasn't worked so far because it always
gives me the worst cold in the history of the
Yuniverse, even prob including people who live on
some really cold and miserable place like Uranus,
pardon me.

Homeopathy was invented by a German doc
called Hahnemann, who thought docs were all

wrong to splash medicines all over the place by the bucketful, and they worked best in V. tiny quantities. This came as welcome news to patients in the 18th and 19th centuries, when Hahnemann was at work, because it was a lot better than having leeches stuck all over yr Bod. It comes as less welcome news to the Western drugs industry in the 20th century, which wants us all to use large quantities of the stuff they make. Homeopathy has been shown to be V. useful in some conditions that can't be fixed in other ways, like allergies Etck, and many people believe in it because it isn't filling yr Bod with dodgy chemicals that may have long-term side effects.

HORMONES

These are chemical substances produced by an endocrine gland and transported in the bludde to certain tissues, on which they have an amazing effect (eg: on boyz' willies Etck). There are loads of hormones buzzing around inside Teenage Worriers, once they start developing sexually. These busy little substances are what make you get urges, cause mood swings, periods, spots as well as Body hair, bazooms and bigger willies. Still, although the little fiends often make us filled with glume, we are better off with them. Cos no hormones = No SEX. Also no HUMAN RACE.

Don't be scared!

Hormones of a Teenage Worrier

IMAGE

Er, THINK (I know it hurts that brain cell) about all that junk in magazines like *Weeny-bop*, *Smirk* Etck that tells you to what to wear, how to do your wig, how much food, exercise Etck Etck you shld be having. What are they saying it FOR? At least with El Chubb's pearls of wisdom you know that she is doing it from the painful experience of a fellow Worrier in the vineyards of Glume. But *Smirk* is just trying to sell more advertising, T-shirts, gunk Etck.

Everybody Worries about their image and poses a bit, say I. If we didn't care at all what people thought of us, we wld prob be V. Arrogant or V. Saintly. Teenage Worriers *have* to do a lot of Posing, it is part of Finding Out Who We Are. It goes like this: dress up in old Tesco's bags held together with Christmas sellotape and boots discarded by giant gas-fitter and found on skip, smear wig with motor oil, stick Granny Chubb hatpin through left eyebrow, hang out singing shouting-song at top of voice. This will divide Werld into those who tell you to Jump Under Bus and those who purr 'wicked' and try to slide hand into Tesco bag.

If you like the people who tell you to Jump Under Bus and don't like the hand-sliders, you have Found Out Something About yerself, and can try another Pose. Eventually you will find a Pose that

50

makes you feel comfortable with Yrself, and Happy
with those you like. Later, of course, when you apply
for Job in Bank, or Lawyers' Office, or supermarket
checkout, you realize you have to start another Pose
to stand any chance of Success. This pose is smiling
a lot and saying 'No Prob'. If this Pose fits perfectly
with yr Inner Nature, you are V. Blessed and
Fortunate Person and not at all like *moi*.

JOSS STICKS

Nice smelly things that look like those little bits of
rafia you used to do weaving with at nursery skule.
Instead, you light these and lie back to inhale
gorgeous perfume. Often used, according to my only
father, to disguise smells of illegal drugges way back
in the 70s.

KARMA

According to Hindus and Buddhists, this is about
all the things you do in this life that will affect you
both in this life and in your next life. Hence, doing
something bad is avoided because it's bad karma,
Etck. Some folks claim to be able to tell if you've
got good karma or not just by looking at you. When
I look at Syd Snoggs in Year Ten, I think I see what
they mean. Arg.

Leonardo da Vinci

Fabulous before-his-time maestro of Science and Art, who united MIND and BODY in incredible drawings of people, pants *(shouldn't that be plants? — Ed)*, water and machines. His most famous pic is the Moaner *(Shouldn't that be Mona? — Ed)* Lisa, but he also drew flying machines centuries before they existed and wrote in mirror-writing in his incredible journals about many things, including the great beauty of the human face at dusk, when the dying light illumines its softness. Ahhhhhhh. I include him, cos it can be V. Inspiring to look at werk of genius and feel amazed that someone with exactly same number of heads, arms, legs, eyes Etck as you cld actually do all that stuff. This shld not make you feel werthless worm by comparison, but give you sense of pride in the grate potential of humanity, ie: that is YOU.

Make-up

Argh. El Chubb's attempt to find perfect stretch-over-yr-own-to-wear-at-parties FACE has so far failed. Even if you could get a really good one, what wd be the point, since no-one wd know who you were the next day and Prince Charming might not

fancy running around with rubber mask saying find
the gurl who fits this? Or maybe he would — in
which case you'd prob run a mile . . .

In the absence of the
ready-to-wear FACE, I
have often dreamt of a
perfect make-up you cld
just roll on that would
do lips, eyes, and rest of
mug in one fell swoop
instead of having to buy
all those dinky little
tubes and cylinders and
packets and then having
to get a little make-up
bag that they can all leak

Just add
scowl

out onto. Naturally, ahem, in a spiritual buke such
as this, one shld be concentrating on higher things,
but now that seven-year-olds are painting their
nails, it is V. Hard to resist blandishments of make-
up ads, with their freshly glowing, glossy-lipped,
shining-eyed, healthy-looking gurlz all grinning out
at you from every page . . . Resist it if you can,
however, and rely, as I do (hollow laughter, sounds
of fingers crossing) on attaining true inner beauty by
thinking good thoughts, eating good food and
breathing good lungfuls of good fresh air (arg,
choke, asthma Etck).

If this fails, get V. Cheap stuff not tested on
animals.

MEDITATION

Both Only Mother and Adored Father have occasionally gone in for Meditation, to contact their Inner Selves, and try to discover if it's possible to share a house with Floor-phobic infants, bazoomless Teenage Worriers, bathroom-monopolizing Romeos, psychotic gerbils, embittered cats, and Each Other without being dragged away to Ye Binne.

In Only Mother's case, this has involved locking herself in the bedroom at dawn and sitting cross-legged on a blanket, going *OMMMMM* until finally surrendering to  the hysterical weeping of Benjy who woke up convinced there was a vast bee in his room. In latter case, Adored Father retreated to The Shed, wrapped himself in a tarpaulin, Got In Mood with two bottles of industrial-strength Trappist Monk lager, and practised deep yoga breathing until he fell fast asleep.

Adored Mother became anxious after a while, searched high and low (including Shed, where she overlooked gently undulating tarpaulined heap in corner) and finally called Ye Bill. Meditating Father finally awoke to find family of woodlice occupying trouser-pockets and stumbled indoors to combined Fury of Only Mother and Vast Policemen issuing All Points Bulletins into radios.

Both of these circs, of course, are stressful enough to need about twice as much meditation to cure the effects as the meditation that started it all in the first place. But many people *do* meditate without these mishaps (it is just a question of finding the right place and time), and research has proved that it can reduce stress, improve the chemical balances in yr Bod, and enhance health. You can either meditate using one of the prescribed methods – there are Transcendental Meditation centres all over the country, and those studying yoga use a series of deep-breathing and focusing exercises to help meditation – or practise simpler, non-religious methods like Mindfulness. Mindfulness was invented by American biologist Prof Kabat-Zinn (it's true, it's true) and is similar to yoga in getting you to listen to yrself rather than constantly thinking of doing something, or Worrying about something you haven't done.

OOMmmmmm mmmm mmmmmm

Nature

Even in ye most blissful countryside there is
usually one who feels ALONE.

One of the greatest soothers for MIND and BODY
is to amble amid waving corn, gazing at fluffy
clouds, with only the sounds of fluffy lambs and the
chirrupping melodies of twinkly birdies for
company, Aaaaaah Meeeeee! Harrrumph, I can hear
the myriad voices of country-dwelling Teenage
Worriers who are forced to stumble about on bleak
moorlands waiting for the one bus every other
month.

You Teenage Worriers who live in the country see us townies as mindless zealots who get all the fun and then tell you off for maiming foxes and breeding mad cows Etck. This is V. True and V. Unfair, especially since townies get all V. Soppy about countryside, just as I do . . . and only use it to waft about in without giving a thought as to what it's actually like to live there. Fact is, country folk have rubbish transport and are often living far from all the stuff we take for granted. (Klubs! Shops! Cinemas! Kulchure! Frendz!)

So, El Chubb's advice for town-dwelling Teenage Worriers is, if you want a complete change, spend a week in the country. And for country-dwelling Teenage Worriers if YOU want a complete change, spend a week in the town. Maybe two weeks is better . . . Everyone will be V. Happy, feel refreshed and stimulated in MIND and BODY and will be V. Happy to return to their own nachural habitat. Er, maybe . . .

OILS
Niff! WAFT! @AROMA

Say YES to Oils and Unguents. Massage them deeply into your knobbly or billowy bod. Roll in them! You can heat them for nice smells, add them to your nosh (er, olive oil Etck, not aromatherapy oils) and know that oil is oiling yourself inside and out. You NEED oil!

Panics

ARGHHH!

Panics, phobias Etck rule our lives more than we know. We all have little compulsions that we keep secret from everybody else (and if you don't have any, you are V. Lucky). To be as scared of floors as my ickle brother Benjy is, though, is to be too scared. I sometimes Worry that maybe he is secretly aiming to be one of those kids who are forced to live in a bubble, as he wants Tabloid newspaper readers to send him teddies Etck. His phobias are not helped by endless Worry heaped on him by my guilty mother. She is sure that he suffers from being youngest, suffers from looking V. Cute and therefore not being taken seriously, suffers from dyslexia Etck. If Benjy is dyslexic then I am mashed otatop, but the middle classes all seem to assume that their boyz are dyslexic if they are not reading Dickens Etck at five, and clearly my only Mother is keen to continue thinking of herself as a toff, despite all financial indications to the contrary.

However, if you feel as engulfed by Worries as Benjy, and that your phobias or weird habitz are a little bit TOO weird and are stopping you living Normal Life (whatever that is) then do go to doc. They will not think you are mad, but they really can provide help for these things, to avoid you ending up like Jack Nicholson in *As Good As It Gets*.

PERIODS

I have writ much about ye periods in my many other tomes, so I have only this to add: Be V. V. Nice to yrself if you have V. Bad periods. Wear long warm tights, take long warm baths, take long warm drinks, snuggle up to long warm boyz (I mean, sofas) and, if poss, strap long warm hot-water bottle to yr middle at all times.

Since Bad Moods often precede Bad periods, you shld start this process a week before yr period is due and continue a week after for comfort's sake. This shld leave you free for one week a month to be 'normal'. Only joking. Honest, this is the kind of advice they used to give gurlz, including things like not swimming and all that. But most of us feel fine during periods. If you don't, see doc. There are V. Good things to help with V. heavy bleeding and cramps these daze.

PRIVACY

Teenage Worriers need privacy. Demand locks on all doors, especially bathroom (ours is always broken and I can hardly sit on loo for five seconds without Benjy barging in waving sting ray lazer gun Etck). Parents go on and on about their privacy but seem to think my life shld be open buke, ie: 'Who was that on phone? What did they want? Where are you going? Look at state of yr wig!' Etck. If I talked to them like that they wld go up wall.

QUALITY OF LIFE

This whole buke is supposed to be about Quality of Life. We all have a Fantastic quality of Life if we compare ourselves to cave persons, or even to Roman Emperors Etck. They did not have TVs, telephones, fridges, blah blah. But there is no definite answer as to whether they were happier or more serene than us.

What you can bet on, however, is that the poor have always envied the rich. El Chubb believes that *Quality* of Life equals *Equality* of life, and will only be achieved when all of us – the clever and the stoopid, even the V. V. lazy – have enuf security to feel dignified and part of society Etck. Until this golden daye, we will suffer either envy cos we haven't got stuff or guilt cos we have. Whichever category you fit in, you know in yr soul that peace of MIND and BODY is what you're after. So CAMPAIGN to change werld Etck, but also to change self and enjoy the fleeting moment.

RELIGION

The subject of Religion is one that causes considerable confusion to *moi*. As a Teenage Worrier I have, naturally, a V. strong desire for Higher

Power to exist. But also as a Teenage Worrier, I
sometimes harbour fears that He, She or It may not.
This wld be sadder than finding out there's no tooth
fairy.

If you have a belief that enables you to stop
wasting time Worrying about the Vast Abyss
Beyond and get on with Life and Lurve, it's a V.
Good Thing. But beware: if you have a belief that's
V. Critical of anything and everybody then it isn't
Good, say I. I must say I have a pref. for Religions
which are Tolerant and Peaceful and that say being a
Yuman Being is a Good Thing and not a Lifelong
Disaster only cured by Banana, Purging In Fires of
Hell Etck.

I espech like the sound of some kinds of
Buddhism (Ommmmmmmmmmmm) because it
seems to *moi* that it can be a way of bringing Yr Bod
and Yr Minde into Harmony, though in the case of
the Bod of El Chubb the two might be better off
keeping well away from each other. But the nice
thing about Religions that encourage Meditation
and tuning in to Yr Bod's energies Etck, is that they
maybe help you to Live more fully in the Moment
Yr Akshully In, rather than biting yr nails about
something you did or didn't do in The Past, or
might or might not do in The Future, and they can
be V. Calming. It is also possible to smuggle these
things into Yr Everyday Life without drawing
attention to them, rather than with more finger-
wagging religions that oblige you to look like

NOT IMPOSSIBLE that bicycles orbit in space...

BUT V.V. Unlikely

Florence Nightingale, or go around with a V. Understanding Maddening Espesh Quiet Voice, or a sandwich board saying in big letters RELIGIOUS PERSON.

They say the more Partickle Physicists Etck find out about all the whizzing, orbiting, colliding things that make the Universe work, the more Religious they get. I'm not surprised. If I spend every day proving that everything in my Life from Adored Father and Mother to Horace are really empty space joined together by flying Bitz and Pieces, I'd need as much Religion as I could get to relieve the Worry of why they don't all fly off in a million different directions and hit the wall. (But of course the wall is a kazillion flying thingz too, aaargh . . .)

RITUALS

MIND and BODY are both soothed by all kinds of Rituals, from religious ones (see above) to comforting ones like always having a hot bath, or a mug of hot choccy Etck. Benjy has about two hundred and twenty little things he has to do at bedtime. I've got mine down to about four . . .

Self-defence

All Teenage Worriers, whether boyz or gurlz, have fear of being jumped on or beaten up in street. Although learning ancient arts of self-defence such as judo, karate Etck cld help to improve yr confidence, they are not infallible, espesh if jumped on by horde of lethal weapon-wielding thugs. No-one can guarantee complete safety, wherever they live, so it is worth bearing in MIND a few simple hints and sticking to them:

* If poss, stick with someone you know when out after dark.
* Don't get drawn into conversations with strangers, just cos you're embarrassed about seeming rude.
* Only carry the dosh that you need for that day/evening.
* Keep to brightly lit, familiar streets.
* Tell your folks/caring adult where you're going and arrange a time to be back by.
* Any hint of an attack, just run like hell.
* If you can't run, just kick, bite and scream for help really loudly.

In films, heroines are always wandering about on above. DO NOT follow their example.

SELF-HARM

If you do this You R NOT alone

It is a V. Sad fact that many Teenage Worriers commit acts of self-harm, such as cutting or burning themselves. Usually, this is done in private and the Teenage Worrier thinks he/she is the only person in the world who is doing such things. It is incredibly important, if you are driven to injure yourself, to try to find help from sympathetic people. There are organizations devoted to helping people who self-harm and who are very clear about getting rid of the myths surrounding it, like it's 'just attention-seeking', or 'It's self-inflicted so it's not serious', or 'If you won't see the psychiatrist you can't want to get better'.

These organizations will not tell you any of the above, but instead will try to understand your particular needs — so if you or a frend are self-harming, get in touch. (See numbers at end of buke.) You will feel less alone and may be able to begin to unravel the reasons why you self-harm — which are obviously different for each individual.

SMOKING

Hey, wow, here's something that smells like barbecued underpants, costs about half what a pensioner has to live on and KILLS you. Buy now!

Fag advertising is actually looking more and more like the above, now that every ad has a warning notice – but obviously Teenage Worriers are attracted to danger, excitement Etck and so even if you plastered the message 'Don't buy, this is timed to kill you, personally, in two minutes' over every pack, it might still not put Teenage Worriers off. A visit to a lung cancer ward might. So might the sight of all the dosh you're going to spend on smoking going up in flames before you. Cos it's true, once you start, it's incredibly difficult to stop (look at my own dear parents). But you know this already . . . Trouble is, Teenage Worriers have many yearnings and if you have V. Deep desire to take V. Harmful substances, you could just be a bit low in energy. Worth indulging in the many nice things to make yr bod feel nice and lurved and cherished that I am advising in this buke and put off smoking until you're thirty. By then, you'll prob be fine without it.

Trouble is, V. SCARY pix like this, ENCOURAGE some of us...

PS: Try kissing an ashtray some time and think what the boy/gurl of yr dreams wd think if *your* breath smelt like that.

SNOW-SAUNA

Snow is just frozen rain, but it seems like a lot more than that. Because it is made of V. Pretty crystals (and not a single snowflake is exactly like any other one, which is a V. Nice Wonders-of-Nachur thought) and it completely changes the familiar werld outside your door so you wake up in the morning and everything looks like picture postcard, children's story Etck, it is one of those magical thingz that is amazing because it's a surprise.

Benjy always hopes it will Snow, espesh at Christmas, but in his little LIFE he has so far hardly ever seen any, and what he has seen turns into stuff that looks like thick mushy carpet of snot pretty quickly. I also remember (though he, fortunately, has forgotten) that in the winter in which he first learned to walk it did Snow, and he went straight out and sank up to his knees in it. Adored Parents clapped hands with glee like in Dick Van Dyke films, laughed at him, took pix Etck, while he wailed piteously and looked like kitten dropped into puddle. This may have been the root of Benjy's prob, we think.

I also remember Adored Father witnessing unexpected blizzard whilst drunk and in the midst of unpredictable mood swings due to ongoing relationship with Trapeze Artist, and flinging off all clothes, plunging into skin-peeling hot bath and then running out to roll around in snow-filled yard, emitting strange chants Etck. He later insisted that this was simply much cheaper than visiting a sauna, and Blessed By Nature anyway, but I think it was the point at which Adored Mother began to suspect something was up with him. So you can see El Chubb looks on the arrival of Snow with mixed feelings. Nonetheless, I will V. Definitely try the snow-sauna on first possible occasion, as long as it is night and the neighbours can't see.

Star Signs

As you know, El Chubb is V. Cynical about horoscopes Etck which does not stop *moi* from reading *ROMANCE in the Stars – the Guide to your purrfect partner* every time they print the same article in *Weenybop*.

A V. New & Exciting STAR SIGN has been discovered: <u>PEGAMARUS</u>. It is a mix of Air and Water and if you are lucky enough to be born under it you will have ability to fly.
(N.B. Don't try this at home).

As a Taurean, I'm supposed to get on well with other Earth signs (Virgo and Capricorn) and have deep and fatal attractions to Scorpios, Sagittarians Etck. How do I know all this if I don't believe a werd of it? Because most Teenage Worriers do. It's part of yoof kulchure among gurlz to drool over horoscopes and even to believe crazed women who write the future in Teen magazines.

NB If you want to prove you can guess someone's Star sign try El Chubb's proven method:

V. Thin person: Libra.

Redhead: Capricorn.

Tearful: Aquarius.

Wearing pink jumper: certainly a Gemini.

Freckles and lop-sided grin: Scorpio

Very short legs with small lumpy feet: Aries

As you see, the above is all B*ll*cks.

NB2 One of my frendz' mums takes all this very seriously and has her own personal astrologer (gulp). I suppose if you spend a lifetime studying it, there might be something in it, but it wd have to be V. personal and not from magazines . . .

SWIMMING WITH DOLPHINS

I bet not a single Teenage Worrier reading this buke has akshully swum with a dolphin — and yet, and yet . . . You wld all like to, wouldn't you? This is one of those fantasies everyone has, of humanity at one

with the animals Etck, and we also have V. Nice
impression of dolphins with their V. Big brains
(bigger than ours) and smiley faces.

Recently there was a story of an eight-year-old
boy who had never spoken. His Mum somehow
scraped together £10,000 to send him for three
weeks to a therapy centre in the USA and he spoke
his first word after swimming with dolphins! Phew.
Even ye most cynical reader will swune with
pleasure at this thought and immediately demand
that dolphin-swimming be included on ye National
Curriculum. Dolphins shld clearly be in charge of all
skules, prisons, remand homes Etck.

If only Prime
Ministers, Head
teachers, Etck
looked more like
this

Pause for a moment while reading, dear Teenage
Worrier, and imagine you are diving deep into
crystal waters with yr dolphin buddy, only to swoop
up again in a cloud of shimmering spray twinkling
in sunbeams. Sigh.

NB It is worth imagining this while you are swimming . . . Not qu. as good as Real Thing, but V. Soothing all the same. AND, if you *have* swum with dolphins, write in to El Chubb, I wld love to hear about it.

T'AI CHI

T'Ai Chi is an ancient Chinese martial art in which you don't do anything martial, ie: you don't actually kick anybody, except by accident.

It's mentioned in a V. Old buke, the *I Ching* or *Buke of Changes*, and comes from the Chinese meaning 'Great Ultimate'. It's supposed to unite Yin and Yang, the passive and active forces in Ye Universe. Now, El Chubb has seen people practising T'ai Chi, which involves a lot of standing on one leg, weaving around like revolving figure in musical box, and usually falling over, and it doesn't look all that Ultimate to me, except maybe the Ultimate Humiliation. However, the path to yr Spiritual Essence is a long one and requires patience, and anything you do as regular exercise, and to put you in better tune with Yr Bod can only be a Good Thing.

UFOS

Vast numbers of people on planet believe in UFOs and, if UFO stood for Unidentified Fallen Object, so wld I, as our floors are littered with them. Hmmmmm . . . little green bit of plastic with knobbly purple attachment. What can it be? Maybe it's from other Werld? Etck.

TAKE ME TO YOUR READER

SKULE LITRESSY PROJICT

I am V. Suspicious of tales of invaders from Outer Space whisking yuman beans away for experiments, however, which seem to be all the rage in the U.S.A. Doubtless, among the zillions of galaxies that we can't even see, there are likely to be other little creatures rather like ourselves, but so far they are keeping V. Quiet, prob because, like us, they haven't invented anything that travels faster than speed of light. V. Exciting though, to hear there is water on the moon. This means there might well have been life on Moon . . . gasp. Have never quite understood why scientists assume that life needs oxygen, water, Etck. You'd think there must be forms of life that have learnt to live by breathing stuff we wld find noxious. And I am not talking about Benjy lying under his covers smelling farts.

VEGETARIANISM

There have been so many food scares recently that a lot of Teenage Worriers have become V. V. Worried about what they eat, leading to an increase in Eating Disorders or just general pickiness. Many Teenage Worriers are turning to vegetarianism as a more healthy and ethical way of noshing. But it's only healthy if you eat enough protein. Campaigning for organic, free range meat is also a good option. The animals have a nice life as well as a nicer taste.

Voice

Dum-di-dum, tarradiddle, tiddley widdly tra la laaaaaaaa.

Singing makes you Happy says Professor L. Chubb,
author of 'BIRDS DON'T GET DEPRESSED'.

When you were a little pre-Teenage Worrier, toddling around yr nursery, you didn't Worry how you sounded, or what noise you made, did you? You cried when you were hurt or sad, you bellowed when you were angry, you laughed like drain when jolly and you SANG. As we get older, sadder, wiser, bogged down with life's adversity Etck, these sounds become controlled and we do, quite literally, 'lose our voice'. El Chubb believes that singing makes you happy. Try it. Just utter a few bouncy notes when feeling low, or hum in the bath. Pay no attention to horrible family saying you can't sing in tune Etck.

AIST

V. Imp for joining berm to top of bod. Try to forget about it otherwise as it is not vis in most Teen Worriers (most will be straight-up-and-down like *moi*, or spherical like my frend Aggy. My other frend, Hazel, moan whinge envy, is unique exception). Waists only used to be teeny in the days of my namesake Scarlett O'Hara when whalebone corsets were used to squeeze waists up into bosoms and down into hips. This was before conservationists stepped in on behalf of whales, thereby doing females V. Good turn and ensuring they started getting good GCSEs instead of fainting in coils.

XTENSIONS (HAIR, WILLY)

Boyz get even more Worried about their willies than gurlz do about their bazooms. And who can blame them? Your bazooms just have to hang about – if you are lucky enough to have something that actually can hang – whereas ye willy has to go up and down, in and out and often does all this with no instruction whatever from its owner and at wrong moments, like when shaking hands with your Mum's boss and glimpsing picture of Sharon Grone over his shoulder Etck.

As for SIZE – well, a 12-year-old boy'z willy is usually between about 3 and 5cm whereas an adult's is between 6 and

V. small (or big) willy within

10cm when dormant and between 12 and 19cm (4 to 7 inches) when rampant. Now you know. Does this help? Are you likely to go around with a measuring tape to check out your lurved one's tackle? Is he likely to? If so, make sure he's careful it's not one of those steel retractable ones that whip back and arrrrrg.

Same goes for bazooms. You've either got them or not, and if you are V. V. Worried about extending same you shld ask yrself why. I did, and the answer I gave *moi*self was: I'd like to have bigger ones, please.

Still, I know I won't have silicone implants Etck. I don't like the idea of all that stuff floating around or poss leaking out. And what wld I be doing it FOR? (To get bigger ones.) There are more important things in life (yes, but what?). Seriously, you know there are.

Of course, extending yr wig is a far simpler matter and good harmless fun. Unless wig is like my own, and breaks into electric frizz at sight of hairpin.

YAWNING

Ever noticed how V. Contagious yawning is? If you Yawn on a bus, ten to one you will notice someone else has caught it. It is grate fun doing this with a frend; Hazel and I once got a whole tube carriage yawning together. While engaging in this harmless merry prank you can congratulate yrself on how good it is for everyone to Yawn. It is a V. Good release of pressure, since lots of tension, apparently, is in our necks and jaws. Yawning lets it out. CAMPAIGN now for more yawning!

Just looking at these pics shld. make you YAWN

YOGA

Omm di om di om di di om
Om di-om-di-om-dee dee
om

Both Only Mother and Adored Father have
attempted Yoga at various times. Adored Father
even went to a class for a while – until (according to
one of Ashley's girlfriends, whose mum went to the
same class) the dreaded yoga farting phenomenon set
him for ever on the lonely path to Higher
Embarrassment.

This is undoubtedly a possible side-effect of yoga
for some inexperienced yogis, and another potential
embarrassment is simply being too stiff to even *know*
you've got some of the places the teacher says you
have to wrap your legs round, let alone being able to
do it. But it shld not put off Teenage Worriers who
are attracted to Yoga, because it is a lifetime study
that can, in time, develop V. Good health and
suppleness of Bod, as well as a reduction in the
symptoms of Worrying, which has to be A Good
Thing.

Some Yogis are supposed to have gained such
complete control over their bodies and minds that
they are not even susceptible to Banana, and live
very long lives. I'm not sure how much of a Good
Thing this is of course, because even though a vast
population of 900-year-old yogis might not eat very
much due to Self Discipline, or use much Fossil
Fuels Etck due to sitting in one place all the time

You've all heard of people chanting OM --but have you heard of HAM, YAM, RAM, VAM & LAM? No, these are not types of tinned nosh, but all YOGA werds. Find yr own CHAKRA and you'll never yearn for illegal drugges, so they say......

OM SWEET OM

Um... Om... YAM... DAMN!

yogi-wogi

Don't try this at home - get a teacher.

going Ommmmmmmm (or possibly getting around by Thought Transference), they still have to have a little patch of earth to sit on somewhere, and if nobody suffered from Banana at all, it would eventually get used up and they'd all have to sit on each other's heads like those motorbike acts in the circus.

ZOMBIE

Zombie comes, according to the Dict. from a West African word 'zumbi', meaning 'fetish'. I don't think this means, however, that zombies are people who go around in rubber flippers, or like being chained up and coated with strawberry mousse Etck, but the orig. meaning of Fetish, which is something worshipped for magick powers. (Well, come to think of it, that's probably what the strawberry mousse people reckon too . . .) Zombies were Ded Bods, supposedly brought back to Life by Ancient Magick, so that's why we use the word to mean V. Slow-witted, dull or inert Person, hard to tell from Ded Bod except by V. Close medical examination.

There have been times when even the V. Nice and Generous-Hearted El Chubb has concluded that Adored Father is a Zombie, but usually when he has consumed aforementioned industrial-strength Trappist Monk lager and then thinks he is imparting V. Imp Deep Truth about The Universe,

ZOMBIES? Nope. Just perfectyl NORMAL Teenage Worriers like U & Me, who have stayed up all night working V.V.V. Hard for insane have-it-all society's vile exams. End this tyranny, sez L.Chubb.

which takes the form of a long, strange noise that goes 'fwwlerrryyuurrnnnnn'.

Whether we use a Werd like Zombie or not, most of us, Teenage Worriers or otherwise, have been tempted to conclude there is absolutely nothing going on inside the Hed or Bod of somebody we know and prob don't like, but Ancient Rune about not judging a book by its cover is worth bearing in Minde. It is also possible that somebody we think is a Zombie and worthy only of ridicule Etck is akshully suffering from Depression (see DEPRESSION) and needs expert help. And another thing – if the Zombie really does turn out to be a Ded Bod brought back to Life by Ancient Magick Etck, it wld be better to stay on the right side of them because from what I hear from Ashley of videos like *Night of the Living Ded* Etck, they're often pretty cheesed off about being woken up.

Which, come to think of it, makes them even more like most Teenage WORRIERS

... And cats

AFTERWORD

And now dear readers, I bid you adieu, *having shared My Inner Worries, bared my Inner Soul, thrown myself on yr mercy Etck Etck, marred only by the sinking feeling (wish I'd never seen that Titanic movie) that I have but skimmed the V.V. tip of the iceberg and that all yr MIND and BODY Worries are still just as Deep and Unsolved and lurking underneath the ocean of yr swelling soul as they were when I began.*

Truth is, Worrying about our lives is part of what makes us human. I hate to admit it, but when I look at Rover, much as I adore her and worship ye ground on which her paws pad, I have to admit that her MIND and BODY and Worries seem confined to:

    a) Food
    b) Sleep

and even in this short list I'm not sure whether Worries are the right description, praps Needs is better . . .

But we humans are always moving the goalposts, seeing greener grass in distance Etck. We want something, we get it, then we want something else. I think there is good and bad in this. If we were all like Rover, I spose there'd be no wars, but also (sigh) no bukes, no paintings, no songs. Moi thinks, the Secret is to be a bit more like Rover, contented in the moment, and try to turn our Worrying bitz into creative bitz. This will prob take the rest of my life.

85

And we ask ourselves, does the purrfect harmony between MIND and BODY exist? My answer, dearest reader, is yes, briefly, for little moments. Now and then, everyone feels that their MIND and BODY are both completely relaxed, but they don't always notice. It often happens when you laugh . . . Treasure ye moments before ye grimme reaper of Glume cuts a swathe of festering pustules through yr bright horizon . . . And also, however deep the troughs of glume may be, remember that your little MIND and BODY will recover, and buoy you up on billowy waves of joy Etck. It's all part of life's rich tapestry.

Yrs truly, madly, deeply (heading for life of quiet contemplation or luney binne, depending on how well I can meditate). Sadly, my own MIND and BODY seem intent on sending large Worry waves through shuddering frame even as I write. Ommmmmmmmmmm. That's better . . . I feel a sneeze — or is it a Yawn? — coming on),

Letty Chubb x

x x x

86

NB. Can you spot difference between this pic and first pic in buke? (Heh! Heh! Cackle Etck.)

Help!

Useful telephone numbers for serious MIND & BODY Worries. There will probly be local numbers, too, in your phone directory. Remember that calls can show up on some itemized telephone bills. And don't forget yr doc shd have lots of helpful leaflets too that can help.

ALCOHOL/DRUGS

Drinkline
Freephone 0800 9178282
(Mon to Thurs, 9 a.m. to 11 p.m.; Fri to Sun, 24 hours)
Very helpful with advice on drinking levels Etck.

Department of Health
National Drugs Helpline
Freephone 0800 77 66 00
A free confidential service open Mon to Sun, 7 a.m. to 11 p.m.
Free leaflets and literature.

EATING DISORDERS

Eating Disorders Association
01603 621414
Youth Helpline
(18 years and under):
0845 6347650
(4-6pm only; recorded message at other times).
Publishes information, newsletters and has details of local services and support groups.

ACNE

Acne Support Group
020 8845 8776

SELF HARM

42nd Street
2nd Floor, Swan Buildings,
20 Swan St, Manchester, M4 5JW
0161 8320170

National Self-Harm Network
P.O. Box 16190
London
NW1 3WW

MIND PROBLEMS

Young Minds
020 7336 8445
Parents Information Service: 0800 0182138
Works to promote the mental health of children and young people.
Can provide advice/leaflets on subjects such as Eating Disorders,
Depression, Bullying, Self-harm Etck.

DISABLED

PHAB
020 8667 9443
Clubs for physically handicapped and able-bodied young people.

SPOD

020 7607 8851
Sex and disability helpline.

GENERAL HELP/
INFORMATION

The Samaritans
National Linkline: 08457 909090 (calls charged at local rate from wherever you call).
24-hour emergency service for the suicidal or despairing. A local number will also be in your telephone book or can be obtained by calling the operator. If in serious trouble, DO CALL.

Youth Access
020 8772 9900
A service for all young people, referring them to independent local counselling services/advice centres Etck.

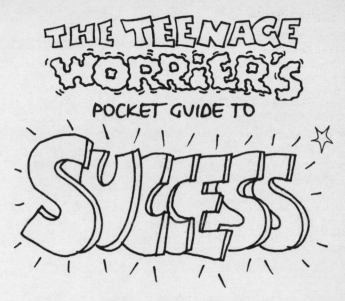

THE TEENAGE WORRIER'S POCKET GUIDE TO SUCCESS

Ros Asquith

as Letty Chubb

CORGI BOOKS

CONTENTS

L. Chubb, striding purposefully towards New Dawn,
Shining Beacon Etck.

Number Ten Downing St
The White House
Vatican
Buckingham Palace
Hollywood
Cannes
Yacht-on-Sea
Champagnesville
Lottery six zillion
I WON 100K
Universe
Eternity

Ye Bluebird of SUCCESS

Dearest Reader(s),

   *As you see from my address above, my new-found
confidence has led me to pen a guide somewhat different
from my other glumcy tomes. This is the El Chubb guide to
having a fantastic SUCCESSful and totally excellent
life-style, starting out with nothing but a couple of dried
peas and a handful of grit. How is it to be done? I hear
you cry. Peasy! Every single thing you need to know is
right here in these dinky pages, pressed like dried flowers
between the leaves of this unbeatable bargain buke. YES!
Within its pages are clues to the following:*

*   *How to get SUCCESS in everything you do.*
*   *How to enjoy SUCCESS when you've got it.*

1

* *How to be a millionaire, world-famous artist/leader/physicist/pianist Etck Etck.*
* *How to be SUCCESSful in Lurve, Money, Friendship, Exams, Business, The Arts, blah blah blah.*

(If you believe all this, dear reader, you are not totally SUCCESSful yet in telling ye difference between truth and falsehood, but since most of our V. SUCCESSful people share this failing with you, you are obviously well on road to same.)

Just a few of the, er, many winding roads to SUCCESS. Each of us has their own path to find. For everyone a different journey... blah, blah, blah.....

Akshully, as you wld expect if you have read my other bukes, you will know that I am not interested in savage, cut-throat, trample-everyone-else-under-feet approach to SUCCESS which Western World embraces. Instead, I yearn for a werld in which each yuman fulfills their hopes and dreams as best they can. And I sincerely hope that in writing it, I will find a way to both help you, fellow Teenage Worriers in the vineyards of glume, as well as moiself, to aim for stars while not minding plunging into pit full of snakes, sulphur and glue every now and then.

If I can do it, being most nervous person in history of Werld, then you can too.

Yrs, full of V. High Hopes (gulp, where's my Lucky Rabbit's foot?)

x   Letty Chubb   x

A FEW SHORT WERDS ABOUT SELF . . .

(for those of you who have not yet dipped into the world of L. Chubb.)

I am a fifteen-yr-old beanpole with hair like spaghetti and more spotz, cold sores and other festering protuberances than any other Teenage Worrier in the werld. I have no sticky out bitz where they shld be, however. I am V. Lucky (I know, though usually forget) to live with two whole parents, although whether the term 'whole' can truly be applied to luny father who barely scrapes living but plays computer gamez all day and Only Mother who was born rich and spends all her time moaning about poverty-stricken state is a debatable question. Am currently dreading GCSEs and writing these bukes to make money so it doesn't matter that I won't get any. I have a V. Clever big brother (Ashley) who all my frendz fancy, but none of his frendz ever fancies me . . . and a V. Sweet-looking but bonkers little brother Benjy, who is scared of floors. My cat, Rover, is V. Old, but she is only person who truly cares about *moi*, I think. Apart from Granny Chubb, who still knits *moi* thingz all the time as though I were a baby, even though she can't see (which is obvious to anyone

4

looking at result of her knitting).

I am in love with Adam Stone, who fails to return my passion. You can read about him and the dastardly Daniel Hope in my other tomes (sob).

I am going to be a film director (notice how confidently I write that, it's part of my new plan: Not 'I want to be . . .' but 'I am going to be . . .').

And now, on with the true guide to SUCCESS . . .

(NB I still say 'banana' instead of that glumey word about dying that rhymes with 'breath'.)

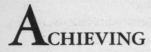CHIEVING

SUCCESS in anything is about achieving and one of
favourite teachers' terms is 'high achiever', 'low
achiever' Etck. But to achieve, you need to know yr
limits as well as yr capabilities. Anyone CAN learn
ANYTHING if they try hard enough. But there's
not much point, in view of El Chubb, in trying V.
V. Hard at things you have zero interest in. You
have to do this at first, to get right number of exams
Etck, THEN find out wot you lurve, and go for
that. Being good at something is 85% work and
15% talent, so not V. Talented people who are
energetic, diligent Etck can do much better than V.
Talented lazy people. (Must raise self from filthy bed
and stretch eyelids).

CTING

I did once dream of acting but my tragic experience
as the Spirit of the Woodland in the Sluggs
Comprehensive panto of *A Christmas Carol* served to
convince me that performance is not my natural
métier. (Incidentally, I often have a Dream that a V.
Handsome Man with Hooded Eyes will come to the
door one day and say he's come to read my métier,
ha ha, however I fear my Adored Mother will get

there first). However, in a play that made Tiny Tim a giant oak tree threatened by cruel woodcutter Scrooge, perhaps I could be forgiven for failing to shine. It may be that I have not yet found the right author to nurture my delicate talent . . . and life on the social security with an occasional end-of-pier performance might at least feel more SUCCESSful than just being on the social security permanently like most of today's yoooof . . . We can but dream.

ADVERTISING

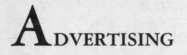

Will this subtle repetition werk?

The tricky thing about advertising is that the Advertisers know we think it's all Krap Etck but the idea is not to get us to believe the message but the message *behind* the message. This can be done by things happening on the screen or in the pic that you hardly even realize are there – or it might be a V. Clever ad that flatters you because it implies you must be Clever to appreciate it, or an ad with characters you get used to so it works like a Soap. However they do it, they're SUCCESSful at worming their way into yr soul. Worth checking out, learning tricks of trade and using for V. Good ends rather than just selling new can of beanz Etck.

Buy another copy of this buke. Buy another copy of this buke. Buy another copy of this buke. Buy another copy of this buke. Buy another copy of this buke.

ANSWERS

Always beware a person, or group of people, who say they have The Answer. There is no one Answer and cultish lunies are likely to lure you into End-of-the-world-style missions that will obsess you, take all your time and may well end up driving you completely nuts. One of the only things I liked about times tables is that, once you learnt them, they always had the same answer. This is V. Comforting, but not true of much else in the werld. There are always many solutions to problems and the SUCCESSful thinker tries to come up with as many as possible and then chooses the best.

APPLICATION FORMS

Campaign for lessons at skule in how to fill these in and how to make the most of yrself, eg: if you have no GCSEs but six younger siblings – 'Very experienced with small children'. This means learning how to be positive without akshully lying.

Name: Letty Chubb
Sex: Not yet (sob)
Age: Fifteen

Arts

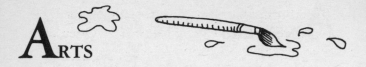

I find that art soothes the turbulent spirit Etck and am probably happier when reading V. Good buke or drawing picture than anything else. I also believe that film is one of ye grate modern art forms and that British film industry under Newish Labour government might have chance to survive. To be SUCCESSful in art, as in all else of any kind, you have to work like maniac. It is not about drifting dreamily and spouting verse, but about trying to express yr feelings about the werld.

Beauty

Although Teenage Worriers think this a vital element in SUCCESS in Lurve Etck, you only have to sit on bus and examine occupants to realize how V. Few of human race actually possess the kind of beauty that we all seem to want. Yet, if you crack joke, you will see each of yr fellow travellers' mugs transforms from leaden inner-city (or deprived rural) mask of glume into V. Nice expression of merriment. This has more to do with beauty of SOUL, naturally, and lots of people have this. If Teenage Worriers cld forget about wanting to be beautiful and concentrate more on beauty around us

10

– little birdies, flowers, grate Art, Etck – then they
wld be happier. And being happy is V. Often the
key to feeling SUCCESSful.

Begging

NB LIFE STATISTIC ALERT: three out of every
five people you see sleeping on London Streets have
degrees (makes you think you should get a job
selling vegetables off the back of a barrow, eh?,
instead of studying Etck. But this is a responsible
buke and must look on Bright Side). Most
SUCCESSful place to beg is apparently the City
(where all the businessmen, guilty lawyers Etck
hang out).

OR, you can sell *The Big Issue*. V. Hard work. Not
for Teenage Worriers with roof over head. But it is
much better to sell something than to beg, as it
gives you some self-respect. Even in incredibly poor
African countries, you usually see someone trying to
sell one old piece of fruit off a box, rather than stoop
to holding their hand out and expecting something
for nothing.

Believing in yrself

It is essential (so I'm told, cringe, wail) to have high
self-esteem in order to be SUCCESSful. Combing

11

tomes about this subject comes up with all the corny old stuff about Standing Up Straight (impossible for banana-shaped person like self) Etck, but L. Chubb has condensed various volumes to give you V. Simple advice:

* Stand up straight (if poss).
* Express yourself.
* Sing really really really LOUD.
* Write lots of poetry about yourself, how you feel, how you look.
* Get your feelings OUT in the open.
* Think about all the great things about yourself and the people you love.
* Tell them. (Wow. Radical, huh?)
* Every time something bad happens, think of its good side if at all poss, or try V. Hard to remember something that is good, even if it happened ten years ago and nothing nice has happened since (wailing banshees, extra mournful violins . . .)

Birthdays

El Chubb's advice for SUCCESSful birthdays: between ages of 13 and 17, forget Birthday parties. Why put yrself through all the Worry of who will come Etck, and whether your parents will wreck it, or how loud the music can be, or whether a gang of gatecrashers the size of bulldozers will come in armed with knives and sell drugs to your baby sister? Instead, just nag your poor suffering folks to fork out a few quid for you to go to cinema or show with yr best frend, or out to fast food joint Etck. Then ask for V. Expensive presents and say how lucky they are not to have the kind of teenager who wants frends stamping fag ends into their carpet (my own parents do this anyway, but some of you probably live with houseproud adults). Then, when you're eighteen, you can get the BIG PARTY sorted out. And no-one can interfere . . .

Books

El Chubb's advice: always have a buke on the go. When Worries crowd in threatening to suffocate the very life from yr glumey limbs, you can stave off the abyss by turning to read of the sufferings, joyz Etck of others. I feel that I shld be reading something a little more, um, sophisticated than the Famous Five, *moi*self, but I got V. Depressed by *Anna Karenina* so am giving self a little break. Thank heavens I did not give *Jill's Gymkhana* Etck to jumble sale.

Despite V. Good SUCCESS-type advice on de-cluttering, (poncey new phrase meaning 'tidying-up'), it is sometimes good for Soul to re-read cosy and comforting bukes that you enjoyed when you were but a happy child without the threatening Worries of impending adulthood, jobz

Etck. Books always tell you that someone has been here before, felt what you feel, Worried about your very own Worries.

I have to say also that, as you get older, you begin to value the ways these things are said too, viz: *I walked along on my own and saw a lot of yellow flowers* does not have quite the same ring as:

'*I wander'd lonely as a cloud*
That floats on high o'er vales and hills,
When all at once I saw a crowd,
A host of golden daffodils . . .'

(That's Wordsworth for all of those who go to skules about as good as Sluggs Comprehensive.) Appreciating langwidge is also V. Satisfying and can feed the Mind, *moi* thinks. It is also the key to SUCCESS in most fields of yuman life. And any of the many thingz I mention in this humble tome can be read about further in grate bukes — all available free of charge at yr local library.

BOREDOM

Is the enemy of SUCCESS. If anything bores you, ask yourself *why*. Is it cos you feel you are too old for it? Or is *it* too old for you? Or it's something you won't need to know about to pursue your chosen career as a belly-dancer? Fine as these reasons may appear to be, you will find that most SUCCESSful people are never bored. They probably started out by running messages, making tea and loads of other so-called 'boring' things and are always looking for hopeful Teenage Worriers that they can exploit rotten just like they were exploited themselves. Ask if you can do the boring stuff and pretty soon you'll find you get to do the fun stuff. If not, move on . . .

Next time you are bored, try to find *one* interesting thing that is happening (it cld even be thinking about why you are bored) and you will magically discover that the sedated sloth of time has turned into the winged hare . . .

L. Chubb sez: There is no such thing as BOREDOM. However, I make exception when encountering above.

BULLYING

It is V. Pathetic to want to hurt other people.
If you identify with any of the above, get help.

TIPS & HINTS
It can be V. Upsetting to be called names: fatty,
skinny, slag, four eyes, smelly Etck are all
wounding, especially if you feel they are true.

Try not to fall into the trap of always returning
an insult, as you can just get into a slanging match
that teaches the bully nothing and drives you crazy.
People who are SUCCESSful and feel happy about
themselves don't waste time slagging off other
people anyway. It's the bullies who have the
problems, and it's nothing to do with you and it's
NOT YOUR FAULT. Here are a few replies you
might like to try out in front of a mirror and then

even try next time someone gets rude. If you can't bring yourself to actually SAY them, then THINK them instead and it shld make you feel better:

'It takes one to know one.'

'The first sign of madness is thinking people with glasses have four eyes. The second sign is saying so.'

'You poor thing, you must be feeling really insecure to say that.'

'You'd never dare say that without your pals round you.'

'Hey! fancy you taking such an interest in the way I look – are you worried about the way YOU look?'

'I am naturally fat (or thin, or spotty, or whatever they said). You, know, like you're naturally rude.'

'Hey! Have you noticed that huge bogey dripping off your hooter?'

'Remind me to borrow you when I need someone to send me to sleep.'

'That's not what you said last night in bed.'

'Thank you for your inspiring remarks.'

'Funny, didn't know anyone with such a big head could have such a small brain.'

'Hang on, could you repeat that so I can write it down?' (This last one shld worry most bullies. They'll think you're going to report them.)

ALWAYS laugh or smile as though you haven't a care in the world. But DO tell an adult if anyone is really getting you down. DON'T suffer in silence.

CALENDAR

What a useful invention for Teenage Worriers!
With a calendar you always know where you are,
viz: to Whit, stuck on the dodgy old earth with a
whole day's Worry ahead of you before bedtime! My
Adored Father sometimes says they managed all
right in prehistoric times without calendars, but
since the days were all pretty much the same (get
up, bash spouse with club, bash passing mammoth
with club for lunch, lie down and have a nap, go to
cave with mates for Happy Hour before sunset, eat
more mammoth, bash spouse with club, go to sleep
Etck) a calendar wld have been a bit superfluous.
However, since organization is basic requirement of
SUCCESSful folk, getting a calendar and writing
your stuff in, is V. Good time-and-motion advice.

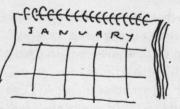

YIPEEEE! Got a
calendar! Booo
hooo! Got nothing
to put in it except
Cat's birthday

CAMPAIGNS

SUCCESSFUL CAMPAIGNING TIPS

1. Choose your subject. Ideally something you feel V. Moved about, rather than just dutiful. Alternatively, you can sneakily choose Ideals of one who is close to your Heart, ahem. Who cares what Adam likes? (And how am I to discover . . . ?)

2. Form campaign group. Rope in Hard-working folk who are prepared to fold and lick things (campaigners always need lots of leaflets, petitions, Etck), but be sure not to phrase yr recruiting pitch exactly like that or you will get a lot of those people who are always responding to ads for French lessons, big chests with fully opening drawers Etck. Try to have at least one person who can spell, as V. Imp to make your points in Literary style. Artistic persons also welcome for logos, heart-rending pics of starving yuppies (sorry, that shld read *Puppies*) Etck.

3. With your group, either join an already existing organization or, if one doesn't exist (frinstance if you are campaigning for something Local), form your own.

4. Name your Group. Acronyms are V. Good here. eg: El Chubb's very own CHAP (Campaign for Hairy Arm-Pits), or a surprising name like ARNOLD for no good reason other than that people will remember it.

5.   Have lots of meetings – V. Good way of asking
V. Handsome (er, dedicated) Boyz to yr house.
6.   Make posters, banners, petitions. Hope Gen
Public does not observe irony of Yr 'Save Trees'
slogans scrawled on millions of bits of paper.
7.   Take same on marches.
8.   Sell old rubbish to make funds (resist
temptation to make this Joke about career path of
Adored Father) Etck Etck.

As you see, campaigns present loads of
opportunities to get out and about and feel useful to
society at same time. Also, if you ARE V. Worried
about the Environment, Animal Rights Etck, then
you can FIND OUT MORE and also DO something
about it.

CAREERS

One big Worry for Teenage Worriers today is that
it's much harder to get good jobs than it was for our
parents, eg: if you want to be a doctor, you already
have to have fantastic A-Levels, have performed
emergency heart by-pass surgery on yr Parents,
starred in *Casualty*, written Hypochondriacs column
in Sunday magazines Etck. And even when you have
all the qualifications, you will often find that you
also need to be grade 8 on the cello to prove you
have 'other interests'. Gaaaaad.

This means you've just got to be V. Dedicated,

hard-werking Etck if you want to succeed in one of the secure professions. At this point, it is werth pausing for a moment to consider what the secure professions are: *Undertaker* is the only one *moi* can think of where one is V. Unlikely to run out of business, although it is hard to imagine a werld that won't need doctors, dentists and (sigh) lawyers, to enable the patients of the above to sue them for taking out wrong tooth, sawing off wrong leg Etck. Wait. *Accountancy* is another well paid, secure job, but *moi* thinks you need more exams for this than you do for undertaking or grave-digging, which only needs muscles. (NB Before training as grave-digger, though, check there isn't a V. Big move to cremation.)

Have just read above and must admit it sounds a bit glumey for a guide to SUCCESS, so will now put on fule's motley and cry from rooftops: try to find something you lurve and then try to think of a way it can actually earn you a living. The jobz situation, which has been V. Glumey for last fifteen yrs (whole of El Chubb's life, sob), is looking better in my crystal ball as I write this – and if you are doing something you lurve, you are much more likely to be a SUCCESS at it. SUCCESS, as you shld by now have realized, is not about fame and dosh, but about feeling good about yrself. And doing anything as well as you can, whether it's painting the yellow lines on the road or exploring Outer Space, can make you feel SUCCESSful.

CINDERELLA

This is a story about apparent SUCCESS which is, in ye humble opinion of El Chubb, a V. Bad example to Gurlz in Today's Society. She slaves away uncomplaining, nagged by V. Nasty Family, being dogsbody Etck. Then marries a prince just because she has small feet! I think such a cynical concoction of anti-feminism and shoe fetishism shld not be held up as a triumph of children's litritcher Etck. And as we all now know, marrying a Prince is not necessarily route to happiness either.

Stuff yer glass slipper. I'm off to be an Astronaut

Naturally, as I may well return to my ambition to be a nun and selflessly serve the community, I do not mean that Cinderella was wrong to devote her life to others, but she cld have chosen some middle course between serving her selfish old bats of sisters and disappearing off to a castle with a prince who is only interested in her below the ankles. *My* heroine is Granny Chubb, who worked V. Hard for a handful of old nail clippings and didn't grumble . . . (but I still think she shld have grumbled more – then she might have a decent pair of specs).

When I am Prime Minister, I will make sure Granny Chubb is rewarded and that Cinderella gets V. Good Edukashun to cast off shackles of Oppression Etck.

COMPUTERS

My Adored Father is V. Bad Example of what can happen if you let computers get on top for as readers will know he is a Hopeless Case of computer slavery to the dreaded computer game. His latest is UNIVERSE, where he plays the person who invented God(!) and creates thousands and thousands of different planets with different eco-systems Etck Etck. Though fun, this is definitely inhibiting him in the SUCCESS stakes, as he wld much rather do that than earn measly crust through writing for a living . . . But we must accept that though computers are throwing a lot of hardworking and decent folk out of work all over the place, they are only tools and it is up to the Moral Values Etck of the Human Race to decide whether they will be an influence for Good or Ill. If we cld only invent a programme to feed everyone in the world for instance . . . Hmmmm.

CREATIVITY

Tapping into this magical force is essential for SUCCESS in most fields. Lots of Teenage Worriers assume that only artists are creative, but in fact creative thinking goes on in all businesses, and in all the sciences. Think how incredibly creative people who are looking for cures for diseases have to be!

Lots of Teenage Worriers think they aren't creative just because they've been told they can't draw or something stupid like that, when they were six, but most of us have a spark in us only waiting to be ignited. A good way to practise this essential discipline is to exercise those brain cells and do IQ-type puzzles, or to think of twenty ways to cross a river without a bridge . . .

How many ways can you find to get from A to B? (The river is deep, and Crocodile infested)

What can you turn this squiggle into? (Repeat, as often as possible, with different squiggles.

This Elephant is standing in front of something. What?

Make up a song, draw a picture or write a story about the elephant, the river, a box of fudge and the squiggle.

INVENT a system of feeding and housing everyone in the world. Send it to The Prime Minister. (or to me - and I'll forward it)

DIAMONDS

Diamonds are often seen as symbols of SUCCESS. Akshully, though I am V. Unimpressed (ahem) with material trappings of wealth Etck, there is quite a good reason for diamonds to have value: they take a long time to form from carbon under deep pressure and huge temperatures in the seething bowels of the planet. SUCCESS, similarly, takes a long time to grow in seething bowels of Teenage Worriers, and is worth nourishing, searching for, and digging up in similar way to diamonds.

When you are a Middle-Aged Worrier, you may have diamonds by the score. (All you need is a diamond mine, thousands of exploited miners, a factory full of sawers and polishers and an absence of guilt!) For now, for *moi*, it's life that matters, not its superficial baubles. I would prefer just the burnished twig that Daniel gave me once with these tender words: *'Letty, when you no longer want to go out with me, you don't have to say anything. Just wear this through your nose and I will know.'* If only he had *meant* it . . .

Documentaries

If you wish to have a SUCCESSful understanding of
the world, you should watch lie-on-the-wall (sorry,
that shld be fly-on-the-wall) documentaries. These
are the serious bits of TV that the BBC occasionally
still puts out after they think everyone has gone to
sleep. They tell you what is akshully going on in
Werld Out There rather than about whether the
latest soap opera star is a junkie or not or whether
two Big Gurlz in American football kit can whack
each other off a high wire with inflatable cucumbers,
and if you are engaging in intelligent discourse
(which of course, if you are reading this humble
tome, you must be) you will need to gen up on info
of this kind, so that when someone asks yr opinion
on whether we shld sell arms to Indonesia, you will
not enquire whether they've had an outbreak of
leprosy in the district.

Dynamism   ZOOOOOM YES!

One of the words most often associated with
SUCCESS. Dynamic people are often thought to be
those who work till midnight, party till 2 a.m. and
are up fresh as daisy with lark to throw themselves
anew into mind-spinning activity of buying and

selling shares, arms factories and small countries Etck. If they are in the arts, they will be the directors of several opera houses and yet still have time to make deep and meaningful films about the true Meaning of Life while dictating their biographies and directing two thousand naked thespians in groundbreaking spectacle based on history of time and space.

Any Teenage Worriers who feel like curling up to die, giving up all hope Etck on reading this should pause to consider that only V. V. V. Few SUCCESSful people are actually this dynamic. There is an inner dynamism that even the average spot-laden, snoozing, slovenly Teenage Worriers can find, and it's to do with tuning in to the thing you like doing best. Frinstance, a boy who is never seen to rise from bed till three in afternoon can transform to whirlwind of activity when put in front of drum kit, Etck.

As a general rule, however, trying to do a *lot* rather than a *little*, is the best rule for cultivating dynamic-type personality. Say YES to new stuff, rather than putting it off till another day, and you cld find strange little strands of dynamism magickally sprouting from yr nut . . .

GO for IT! YES!

YEAH Woooooooosh!

EMOTIONAL INTELLIGENCE

Hey, I understand

This is a new catchy werd for wot the mothers of the human race have been doing for centuries – that is, responding intuitively to other members of human race and negotiating pitfalls of loathing, cruelty, glume Etck by understanding human frailty and avoiding its worst excesses. Developing Emotional Intelligence is obviously hard for those apparently born without it (I name no names, but many werld leaders seem to be afflicted this way), and there are several bukes about that are worth dipping into to see if you've got it or not. Obviously it is possible to be rich and powerful without it (in fact, it may be obligatory not to have it) but if you want a SUCCESSful life as imagined by L. Chubb, which means a happy and fulfilled one, then this is for you.

I think we'll have to cultivate his EMOTIONAL intelligence

2+2

ENVIRONMENT

Looking after the planet is going to be the key to the SUCCESS of humanity's survival or not. Therefore, going into any form of ecologically friendly work is going to be good both morally and in terms of your own SUCCESS as a member of Yuman Race. Even big banks and werld conglomerates are now being forced to take a bit more care of the werld and the voice of every humble Teenage Worrier can make a difference. So: CAMPAIGN for organic food, clean fuel, saving water, cancelling Third world debt (where poor countries are spending more on paying back rich countries than they are on feeding their own people!) and other V. Good things. SUCCESS, predicts L. Chubb, will surely follow.

Exams

Sadly, the passing of exams is seen to be essential for SUCCESS in today's cruel grinding werld. It is V. Important to try V. Hard to do this while at the same time realizing that many SUCCESSful people were NOT good at skule and flourished in the even crueller market-place of life by using different parts of their brains and body. In El Chubb's talent-frendly Yuniverse, you should not need exams for art skule or music college or drama skule or sport – all you should need is to be good at these things and full of enthusiasm. But unfortunately you DO need exams. So, to pass them:

EL CHUBB'S EXAM TIPS
1)   Revise V. Hard in plenty of time.
b)   Ask your teacher what bits you need to work on most.
3)   Do the most and best coursework you POSSIBLY can.
D)   Get a V. Good 'How to pass exams' style guide – there are loads of these about.
e)   Read the questions carefully.
f)   Be sure to answer the right number of questions.
7)   Do the bits you are confident about first and then go back and fill in the others, but be sure to leave time.

8)   Go to bed V. Early and eat V. Healthy food for two weeks before big exams start.

9)   Do not despair if you do badly. You have yr whole life ahead of you and these horrible daze will seem like nothing then (so they say, arg Worry Etck). Seriously, there are many tragick cases of Teenage Worriers being pushed so hard by themselves or, more likely, by Middle-aged Worriers, that they completely freak out over exams. The key to SUCCESS here, is to do as above and then RELAX.

Phew. Summer!

FEELINGS

Adults always say that growing up SUCCESSfully is about getting your feelings and your judgement balanced so they don't keep going up and down like a seesaw. But some Middle-aged Worriers, espesh the ones you read about in the papers who order terrible things to be done in wars, or keep people in prison just for disagreeing with them, or even just fire people who've worked for them for years, or fax messages to their BeLUVREds saying sorry but they've met somebody nicer, don't seem to have any feelings at all, or if they do they keep them locked up in one part of their lives and don't let them spread around and get in the way.

34

Which is why in my less Worried moments I'm glad I have a lot of Feelings, even if they're often a Nuisance. I spend a lot of time and energy not just Worrying about *moi*self, but about how other people are feeling about something I've done or want to do, and maybe when I'm older I won't Worry about that so much and leave them the room to make their own minds up without me doing the Worrying for them. But without all these feelings sloshing about, you wouldn't be able to feel happy about yr SUCCESS, would you? Or the SUCCESS of people you lurve? All you would have is a kind of tarnished gloating, so wot wld be the point?

FRIENDS

There are Middle-aged Worriers and Teenage Worriers on the planet who call themselves sociopaths. These are people for whom frendz and frendship have no meaning and I am not one of them. These people are often V. SUCCESSful in a way, as they have never been hampered by the feelings of others but have just gone their own sweet (or sour) way. They have loads of time, too, as they are never on the phone for hours to someone who has just been left, sacked Etck. They are the ones who *do* the leaving and the sacking. If this is the kind of SUCCESS you want, then you are probly reading the wrong buke.

If you are fond of other people but worried that they do not return yr feelings, first check out that they are not sociopaths. If they are just ordinary Teenage Worriers, then smile hopefully, show an interest and you may find they like you too. There's no point in trying to be frendz with everyone – that wld just make you like a little dog that wags its tail pathetically whenever it's patted. But having a few really close frendz is V. Good for a SUCCESSful life in the opinion of El Chubb, even if it does take time away from being grate artist Etck.

Everyone has moments when they feel rejected or alone but it is V. Sad when the ones you wish to engage with you in the rich tapestry of life are indifferent to you. It does not mean they dislike you, simply that they do not really notice you – or are just too busy with their own lives. If, despite all your wiles, manoeuvres Etck, the Frend of Your Dreamz still says 'Hi, it's great to meet you' when you're in the midst of initiating yr sixth conversation with them that week, give it just one last try. Wear Outfit opposite (whether you are a Boy or a Gurl). No response from your Dream Frend means Indifference. Retire gracefully and seek Partners new.

Part of a decent SUCCESS plan is learning to take the slings and arrows of indifference on the chin. (I don't know why they say 'the chin' – the slings and arrows seem to hit me in all parts of the Bod at once). If this was all our chins had to put up with,

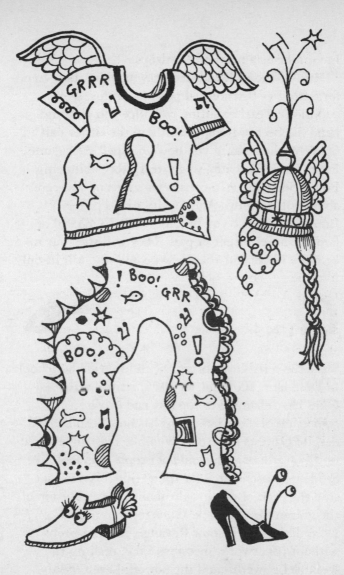

If you seriously consider actually wearing this,
you may qualify for
a) Lottery grant for the Sartorially Challenged.
b) Medical Attention.

life might be a bowl of peardrops.

Run-of-the-mill indifferences includes: Best frend forgetting yr Birthday (if parents do this, seek adoption); Teacher failing to notice you although yr hand has been waving pitifully in the air for half an hour; Mother asking you how you spell your name Etck. This is just life, so get real, stop whingeing Etck. (Boo hoo.) Almost always someone you care about will turn up. And loyalty to old pals is V. Imp. If by chance you become V. SUCCESSful or famous, never forget yr pals. They will turn out to be more important than new people who might only like you cos you're rich.

G<small>UNS</small>

Since the terrible shootings of children at the school in Dunblane, Scotland, in 1996, attitudes toward Guns have changed in the UK and private ownership of most handguns has now been banned, despite protests by people who like blasting away at birdies, cardboard cut-outs of people who look like Saddam Hussein Etck for sport. But this does not stop the prob of what to do about the celebration of the gun in Movies Etck. Guns seem to fulfil V. Deep desires for Instant Revenge, settling probs without paperwork, meetings Etck, making the weak feel powerful and the powerful even more powerful. Worse still, it is poss at times to sympathize with these feelings. But I dread to think what might have happened if the only kind of SUCCESS you could have would be at the end of a gun. Banning all guns is a hopeful dream of L. Chubb. But who knows, if our generation Teenage Worriers can get SUCCESSful enough to rule werld, maybe we can get rid of them for good? We can only try . . .

HAPPINESS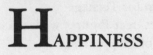

Happiness is something the Yuman Race strives for. Although impossible to identify except when you are experiencing it, it is thought by many to be the key to a truly SUCCESSful life. People look for it in different ways, and believe different things are stopping them from getting it. Benjy strives for Happiness by not stepping on the floor if he can help it. Horace (Benjy's hamster) strives for Happiness by going round in his wheel (his potential for Happiness is of course somewhat more restricted than his Ancestors, by being shut in a cage all day). Rover seeks Happiness by rubbing your leg until you've found the tin-opener, and then going to sleep. Adored Father strives for Happiness by dreaming of Writing His Novel but akshully spending all his time walling himself in, banging nails through his toes Etck, believing that in the midst of this Chaos, Swearing, Collapsing of DIY

Projects at approach of the first feather-duster Etck, lies an Inner Peace in which a man is Absolved By Honest Toil.

It's V. Dangerous to criticize other people's ways of Seeking Happiness, unless their idea of a Good Time happens to be World Domination, Raping, Pillaging Etck, which of course for many of the Most Famous and SUCCESSful Names in History it is. (This of course is a problem for Teenage Worriers, viz: so many of the Great Figures we learn about have such a weird idea of Happiness.)

However, dear Readers, have you spotted the Fly in the Ointment, the open manhole cover in the Journey of Life, the Iceberg threatening the blissful course of Leo and Katie?

You gottit. If everybody's Idea of Happiness is so different, how can every Yuman Being SUCCESSfully find much as possible of their own version without stepping on other people's? It wld make *moi* V. Happy to swear Undying Lurve and Devotion to Adam Stone but in my more sensible moments I have to consider a V. V. Tiny element of doubt that He might not feel the same. It might make *moi* Happy to grow a vast Tropical Rain Forest at the bottom of the garden full of exotic Boids, chattering monkeys, gerbils the size of badgers and strange undiscovered tribes who play wild, Urge-Awakening music that reunites you with yr Primal Being, but it wld not make Adored Parents happy when they get the letter from the Council, and the burning stake on the door from the neighbours.

Happiness is therefore a balance, between yr own needs and those of others. This is not to say that your Search for Happiness will not sometimes cause pain to Another (such as when you have to tell Eric Grovel in 9L that despite his Smile of Hope and geyser of perspiration when he sees you, and Valentine cards every day of the year, you think the two of you shld be Just Frendz) or that you may not occasionally need to be tough to be fair on both them and you. It's just that if you make a Habit of it, you may have an underlying desire to cause Unhappiness that can sometimes be caused by not liking Yrself as much as you think you do – and if that's the case you, or you and somebody who understands, shld maybe ask why.

Health

It is V. Hard to be happy, or even slightly serene, or SUCCESSful in any way, if you feel ill all the time, so eating well, exercising a bit, sleeping enough and not poisoning yr bod with evile crazed drugges is V. V. Imp.

If you feel that you are excessively Worried about yr health and go to doc's thinking you have brain tumour Etck every other week or find yrself looking up 'sore throat' in book of symptoms and convincing yrself it's meningitis, you could, just possibly, be a hypochondriac. I shld know (blush, guilt at bothering NHS who shld be caring for terminally ill pensioners. And did they *really* check that pimple out? Could it be a . . . tumour!? Etck). Try V. Hard to make yourself forget about these Worries for a year. You can do it (I've managed not to consult dictionary of symptoms for eight whole daze so far and am feeling much more Worried, I mean, much better for it).

Hobbies

Moi, I find that a SUCCESSful cure for Worry is when I'm involved in hobbies. When I was nine, it was collecting model horses and making little saddles and bridles for them. When I was ten, I briefly involved myself in forgery (fivers, stamps, old

letters that I tried to sell to newspapers pretending
they were from Stalin Etck). And my lurve of
football was legendary and V. Sadly nipped in bud
by absence of opportunity and constant heartless
jibes about my resemblance to goal-post Etck
(whail, gnash, renting of nets Etck). But small
SUCCESS in hobbies can be V. Rewarding, whether
it's finally completing that 50,000 matchstick
model of the *Titanic* or hand-rearing stag beetles. Go
for it.

H<small>OPE</small>

Essential ingredient for SUCCESS. Must cling on to
shred of same, even when in deepest glume at failed
SUCCESS, for there is always a new day Etck. Each
time you get up, there is new HOPE; each time you
open envelope, answer phone, open door Etck there
is new HOPE. Each time you go out of house, you
HOPE you might turn corner to see person-of-yr-
dreams Etck. Do not approach postman in this
frame of mind however as he is prob married with
seventeen children. My frend Aggy's mother ran off
with postman causing tragick family breakdown
Etck.

Ideas

IDEAS from the Teenage Think Tank.
Teenage Women have best inventions
(but least dosh).

IGNORANCE

Huge and deadly force that deprives world of life-enhancing spirit. True enemy of SUCCESS of all kinds. This is not just to do with bukes Etck but to do with understanding different people and cultures. It is the lack of understanding, and lack of listening, which as all Teenage Worriers know, is a V. Common fault with most Middle-aged Worriers, that leads to ignorance. The SUCCESSful blotting out of same can only be achieved by the exercise of . . .

IMAGINATION

Without which, no true SUCCESS is possible. You must be imaginative to understand problems and therefore solve them. You need imagination to write, to paint, to make anything at all. And it's making things that makes us who we are.

IMPERIALISM POWER DOMINATION and other V. Bad stuff

This is what Big SUCCESSful Nations do to little Nations. They conquer them first, and then try to squash all the thingz their people do that are different, so they might one day feel that giving all their best stuff to the big nation is just like keeping it in the family. But it never completely changes the minds of the conquered people, as the Romans found with us, and we found in doing it to lots of other people. The decline of the British Umpire has been sharp in recent years and it's amazing how well all the little Nations hung on to their traditions against the odds. This is not the kind of SUCCESS, I hardly need to say, admired by L. Chubb.

But Imperialists are cleverer now. Instead of taking over with Guns, whips, general Bossiness Etck, it is now done with Money. The USA for instance has V. Big Influence around the world not just because it has the most powerful army (though it does) but because people want Levi 501s, Mad Mikie Jackson records Etck, all the way from Bolivia to Bangalore. Investment or no investment by multi-nationals can now make or break little countries, as unconventional but V. Poor places like Nicaragua have found. A SUCCESSful world, such as most idealistic Teenage Worriers wld like to inhabit, will attempt to reverse these injustices, led by the Duchess of Chubb, naturally (I may find it in my heart to accept a title if House of Lords not abolished by the time they offer me one. Although I shall naturally do so with um, modest reluctance).

INTELLIGENCE

My big brother Ashley has loads of this and me and Benjy seem tragickly to have the mouse's share. My Only Mother wrings hands and wails, as she thinks it is cos Granny Gosling forked out to send Ashley to a posh school and she has therefore let her only daughter down. I agree that class sizes of about six little chaps with V. Pushy parents, tuba and yoga lessons Etck probably gave Ashley an advantage over *moi* but this is *education*, not *intelligence*. (I do have sneaky suspicion, however, that number of brain cells doled out by genetic inheritance Etck was V. Unfair, so that when Ashley got purrfect face, body, soul Etck, he also got more generous share of grey matter. If he weren't so V. Kind and understanding I wd hate him.)

EL CHUBB'S INTELLECT LIFE-TIP
Try to develop as much of the IQ-type intelligence
that passes exams as you can. Choose the subjects
best suited to your type of intelligence. Never mind
that the exams are V. V. V. Narrow measurements,
cos you need to pass some of them in order to get
into a position of power from which to change them.
BUT don't kid yourself that passing them makes
you a Better Person or that people who don't are
somehow worse than you. If you do, you'll forget all
about changing them and start to think that the
system works . . .

And try to develop as many other kinds of the
other intelligences as you can — creativity, intuition,
Enquiring Mind Etck. This will develop you as a
whole and decent person who is capable of thinking
fast and empathizing with those who don't.

Jobs

Fewer people in the UK are being more industrious
than ever before, I reckon — in other words, running
as fast as they can to take care of jobs that used to be
done by three people and are now done by one V.
Baggy-Eyed person and a desktop computer they
could have run the moon programme from a few
years ago. These changes mean that industry in the
other sense — factories and stuff — is now in a V.

Sorry State in Little Britain, which is why so many people are V. Depressed and why Teenage Worriers are more Worried than their parents used to be at the same age, cos there are likelier to be fewer jobs in the future, unless Govt follows advice of Teenage Think Tank to share out werk properly.

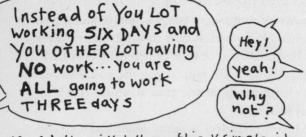

N.B. Adults will tell you this v. simple idea won't work. But **WHY NOT?**

Multi-national companies now look at the world map and don't see people like you and me and our Adored or Appalling Parents but markets, and wage-costs; so they move businesses where they can get the job done most cheaply. Teenage Worriers now have to contemplate New Questions of Our Time like does it mean anything to be British (or French, or Dutch, or Eskimo), and how can I figure out which life Skill or Skills will be worth anything in the year 2010? If you have any answers to these Brain-Hurting issues, please contact the El Chubb Think Tank.

See also CAREERS. Which leads us naturally to . . .

JUGGLING

I do not mean clubs or balls, but juggling loads of
different things at once (feeding Rover, getting to
skule, placating worries of Only Mother, Benjy
Etck, surveying spotz – my life is a nightmare of
conflicting demands). Learning how to do this well
is obviously wot differentiates the truly SUCCESSful
Teenage Worriers from the slobs like *moi*. Must
make list . . . argh, hopeless case, Worry. Etck.

KNOWLEDGE

Getting as much of this about as many things as
possible is essential for SUCCESS. But getting a lot
of it about one thing in particular is the key to
mega-SUCCESS. Once you decide what you really
want to do, you can not bother to learn about things
you don't like. Sadly, when you are a Teenage
Worrier you need to dip into everything as it's only
by doing that that you can find out what you
DON'T want as well as what you do. (At least I
know for sure that I'm not going to be a pilot or a
ballet dancer, so that's two things I can cross off vast
list.)

I'll just give little eg of knowledge: let's take, say,
(she says, pretending to pick something at random,

51

but akshully going for own little obsession), *Horses*.
If you want to show SUCCESSful knowledge about
horses, harken to this: they are measured, not in cm,
km or even feet and inches, but hands. Weird, huh?
Their saddles, bridles, and other taming
paraphernalia are all called Tack (which is short for
tackle). When you brush them, it's called grooming
and their hairbrushes are called things like Dandy
brush and curry comb. So . . . if you hear some
hearty type saying: 'Jolly fine filly, about 15 hands.
Just off to get the dandy, the curry and the tack',
you'll know what they're on about and won't think
they've discovered some great new take-away caff.

I make this point cos this is one of the few things
I know about. But it is easy to find out about
anything you're truly interested in so, for 'horses',
just substitute 'planetary systems', 'violin music'
Etck and go and FIND OUT. Learning about
ANYTHING AT ALL is key to SUCCESS.

LAUGHTER

If you can cast cares to winds, make light of heavy
sorrows, laugh through yr tears, put on happy face,
whistle happy tune, smile though yr heart is
breaking Etck, you will stand better chance of
SUCCESS in Life's journey Etck.

'Laugh and the World Laughs with you' may be a
V. Good Saying but sometimes, a chuckle will do.

LIQUORICE

You may think you can skip this entry, but
SUCCESSful life lessons come in surprising places,
so read on. (Write in and complain if I am wrong.)
Liquorice is a ghastly sweet, the extinction of
which would not diminish the quality of life. If
only the energy that goes into the making of
liquorice went into the making of FUDGE then the
werld would be a happier place. But wait, what is
that distant cry? It is the cry of the *Glycyrrhiza
glabra* farmers, whose leguminous plant forms the
root from which liquorice is made. The gooey stuff
also goes into medicines. Which goes to show that
whatever you think, there is usually another point
of view.

The apple the cloud the Kangaroo
Each has a different point of view

LOTTERY

Of course winning the Lottery wld make *moi* happier, but then I am a Teenage Worrier and we know what imaginative World-enhancing things we wld do with all that lovely dosh. The adults who win seem to just get more of the things that made them depressed in the first place – bigger houses to keep tidy, more sofas to worry about the colour of, vast gardens to fret about the weeding of, more slaves to moan about the unworthiness of . . . yachts they don't know how to sail or fix, holidays where they get sick of the food and sea-sick and home-sick. Then there's all the law-suits from ex-wives and children they never knew they had, old frendz they haven't seen for twenty years asking for a little something to tide them over, begging letters Etck, Etck.

MANNERS

Being polite is obv helpful in being SUCCESSful. Nobody likes rude young bats who shoulder them aside at bus stops Etck and although the world of Middle-aged Worriers is full of such people who got big by being bossy, El Chubb believes (or at least hopes) that Teenage Worriers will build a werld

where people can be both SUCCESSful AND caring.
'Manners don't cost anything' says Granny Chubb.
If only today's yoof could educate their parents
about this, how much better and more dignified a
world it wld be . . . sigh. Even so, I bet Hitler knew
how to use a knife and fork, so manners are not a V.
Good guide to the SOUL.

MARTIAL ARTS

El Chubb has often wondered, it has to be said, what
all this eastern Bruce Lee stuff, like ballet with
muggings, has to do with being a Better Person,
becoming more sympathetic to old ladies, working
out why yr family are all Psychos Etck. However,
that's the very Prob. In the west, we spend all the
time we aren't out causing havoc, intervening all
over the place, making Big Decisions Etck, trying to
work out in our Hedz how we can do Better
Intervening, make Bigger Decisions and so forth.
But in the eastern philosophies of Taoism and Zen
Buddhism, they reckon you should spend all the
time you currently spend thinking, practising how
to be better at *un*thinking instead. Then yr Body
and yr Mind Become One, so that in combat you
instantly respond without thought, and all other
times like going to the Loo, cleaning the gerbil-cage
Etck, you are in a spiritual state of balance in which
there isn't a You inside and a World outside. I have

to say that if the contents of above gerbil's cage are akshully part of *moi* rather than disagreeable elements of an External World then I may end up a bigger Teenage Worrier than I am now, but perhaps it's unwise to go into the details of these things.

BUT if I cld achieve this balance it wld obv be V. SUCCESSful in terms of self-defence, a vital need for today's Urban Teenage Worriers.

Money

Dear Mum
I Berrid yor £$5
in the GarDEN cos
yor arlwais saing
You wisH yor muny
WOUld gRo
LOV
Benjy X

Just one of my beloved family's
many financial disasters.
The fiver was never found.

If you have opened a bank account you will now
know that Staff in banks spend a lot of time wishing
you a nice weekend, apologizing for the delay,
sweeping red carpet before Yr every step Etck, but if
you owe them the equivalent of a drop in the ocean
of their hoarded zillions that they weren't expecting
you to owe them they change V. Quickly and
tell you to cough up or they'll get the ladz round to
nick yr video. Banks, though, are now V. Imp to
students because the Govt has encouraged them to
finance student loans which means that for half of yr
life you are working for them instead of for Yr
Dreamz, nearest and dearest Etck. This is all part of
a conspiracy called the World Banking System, in
which the same principle is applied to developing
countries very like El Chubb. The World Banks
basically give student loans to poor, undeveloped,
snuffly-nosed, skinny countries like *moi* to encourage
them to learn how to be big, glossy, shiny-nosed,
respectable countries like my posh frend Hazel's
dad. The little countries aren't sure how to do it, or
sure if they want to, so the Banks demand about
twenty times their money back to help them
concentrate, and encourage multi-nationals to build
factories there so that they can get lots of cars,
computers Etck built for tuppence. To get everyone
a fair bite of world's cherry, we have to stop all this
rubbidge and not ask for our money back. SUCCESS
means giving up as well as getting.

The search for money of your own, though, is

something of an obsession for Teenage Worriers, espesh if like Hazel, you are surrounded by rich kids who all get allowances from their V. Rich Paters and Maters (this is Latin for parents, as Ashley has often pointed out to poor ignorant, comprehensively-educated *moi*). But I am determined to make own dosh and not rely on hand-outs, from parents or anyone (chance wld be a fine thing with my parents anyway, wail, moan, cries of 'It's not fair' Etck). Am trying to revive old hobby by forging old-looking fivers as we speak, with help of V. Good new computer programme that scans notes and prints them out. V. Hard to get watermark right . . .

NB If you want to both understand money and make it, Accountancy is a career worth considering as Accountants are for V. Rich people to help them avoid paying money to the Government to educate the likes of *moi*, Build A Just Society Etck, and save up money to educate the likes of themselves, Build A Vast Mansion with Three Swimming Pools Etck. Hence, if you become an accountant you will have big cheques from rich people as long as you can kid them you are helping to make them richer.

Please don't get
IMPRESSION I am
OBSESSED with
MONEY. I just like
to doodle (blush)

NEGATIVITY

If you have V. negative 'glass is half empty' as opposed to positive 'glass is half full' attitude to life it may be hard to entrap the elusive glimmerings of SUCCESS.

My own family is V. Dysfunctional in this respect as we are all whingeing victims of Fate, except Ashley. Hence: Only Mother moans about how she used to be swimming in dosh until she married my penniless father. Adored Father moans about how nobody understands the travails of a working class novelist who had to look after his penniless mother. Benjy moans about the floors, the dark, the light, school, food, his clothes Etck. And I am as you know V. Put upon having a father who won't werk, a mother who won't cook and a brother who won't shut up. Am making V. Big resolution to look on Bright side Etck and pursue goals in orderly fashion blaming no-one but myself if I go wrong. If I'd been brought up in sane family it wld be much easier, moan whinge, there I go again . . .

Half Empty?   or   Half full?

NEW THINGS

Embrace the New! Also embrace the old! But do not be scared of things. I only wish I had been taught to try out new stuff instead of being lumbered with a neurotic mother who told me to be careful every time I went outside the front door . . . New experiences, as long as they are legal, are almost always rewarding Etck. Even if you don't fancy scuba diving, if you get the chance, go! (But do not embrace the shark, er and remember to wear a wet suit and . . . Worry, worry)

OYSTERS

V. Expensive 'delicacy' eaten by SUCCESSful people with more money than sense (as Granny Chubb wld say). I wld never eat an oyster after reading *The Walrus and the Carpenter* because I cld never forget Lewis Carroll's haunting lines:

'What think you, little oysters?'
But answer came there none.
And this was scarcely odd because
they'd eaten every one.

The betrayal of Trust in this great pome seared my eleven-year-old heart when first I read it and has left its mark for eternity. I draw the line at white-bait, too. Too many little lives in one mouthful.

Phones

Brrrrrrrrrr Brrrrrr

Mobile phones are always carried by people who want to look SUCCESSful. V. V. SUCCESSful people do not need them however as instead they have a faithful army of minions who answer all their calls for them. I hope to be one of these before too long (not the minion, the SUCCESSful person). But does this big improvement in ability to commoonicate make us Happier and more SUCCESSful people? Discuss.

Sound makes me SHIVER with anticipation. No wonder th

TIP
If desperate or broke (or both!), you can always borrow small sibling's toy mobile phone which has V. Convincing ring.

Poetry

It is V. Touching that so many Teenage Worriers write poems and it is V. Good for the soul to do so, but – I hate to say this – not many of the poems are actually V. Good. You only have to read some of those middle-aged Worriers poems that are printed up in real-look leatherette by cheapskate publishers and then sold to the authors for £35 to see that this is not a talent that necessarily improves with age. If you want to impress and are not too sure of your own skill, why not use a poem from one of the Truly Grates? You can go for ye Big Old names: Shakespeare (lots of love sonnets, many of them to a boy if you want poem for yr BeLurved), Marlowe Etck, or try more modern stuff like Roger McGough, Benjamin Zephaniah, Murray Lachlan Young Etck. There are loads of collections.

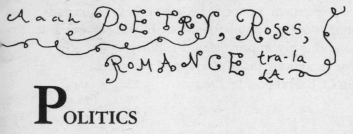

Aaah POETRY, Roses, ROMANCE tra-la LA

Politics

Really SUCCESSful Politicians are Good Listeners, sez El Chubb. I reckon they're the ones who can hear what people different to them are talking about (Teenage Worriers, frinstance, but also poor people, those speaking different languages Etck Etck) and balance it against all the other Stuff going on in Society, so the Laws Etck reflect the needs of as many people as Poss. So if you want true SUCCESS in politics, rather than just crude old power, this is what you shld be like.

Just a few
questions *

* <u>Samples:</u>

1 When did you last queue for
   a bus?

2 When did you last pick your
   kids up from school?

3 When did you last wash a
   sock?

4 When did you last wash a
   pair of socks?

5 Do you think financial
   advisers should earn more
   than nurses?
   (Etck. Etck. make up your own)

Positive Thinking

LIFE-TIP: If you feel you have a tendency to look on down-side, remember El Chubb's two fave sayings: *Life is just a bowl of Cherry stones* and *When one door closes, another door closes.*

If you can do better than this, award yrself small life-enhancing treat ie: a single Smartie.

My dad Killed my Mum. I've had 19 Foster families. I'm due in court on Monday. I've never had a Best Friend or a pet and I've never seen the sea. BUT, the sun is shining, I have a pen, paper, shampoo, food. I am definitely better off than V. Big number of people in the world and I am going to IMPROVE EVERYBODY'S LIVES

Er, this Teenage Worrier is V. Good example of Positive Thinking (guilt, writhe, mone...)

PULLING STRINGS

Er my cousin's friend's aunt's daughter worked for you five years ago and suggested I give you a ring

SUCCESSful Middle-aged Worriers often call this networking, which is a polite way of saying they go to parties Etck in order to toady up to more SUCCESSful people than themselves in case they need them later. Obviously, if you have rich SUCCESSful parents who can put a word in the right ear of bank manager, werld leader, newspaper editor Etck you are in with a much better chance than the majority of Teenage Worriers who have to bumble along making it up as they go. I think this is V. Unfair, but then life often is V. Unfair and will continue to be until werld is run by *moi* (power-mad visions of domination Etck).

So, if you have frendz or contacts of any kind in the kind of jobz you are looking for, it does make sense to get in touch. People like to work with people they know, and will be V. Likely at least to give you a small opportunity to show what you can do. So don't be shy of pulling strings if you are lucky enough to have any to pull (sigh, chance wld be a fine thing Etck).

QUESTIONING

SUCCESS depends on asking the right questions at the right time, viz: if I drop this heavy weight on my foot, will it ruin my chances of being footballer? Without the ability to ask and answer questions, you will not get far down yr chosen path. Questioning also means not just accepting the answer you're given, viz:

Can I have a job?
No.
Why?
Because you're not suitable.
Why not?
Because you're too stupid, young, inexperienced, lazy (Etck).
Why do you say that?
Because it's true.
It's not, let me show you.

NB Confidence is necessary for above. Practise in front of mirror and don't take no for an answer.

68

Racism

If you feel yr SUCCESS in finding work or frends is due to your colour, you shld immediately report it to Race Relations authorities. There is obv no hope of a SUCCESSful country that goes on discriminating against people for these krap reasons, but it does still happen. If you suspect it, always ask why? The person who you think is being racist will be V. Embarrassed if it's true.

← unless they believe what some other V. stupid person has told them. Why not see if they agree with the signs above

Rewards

You need rewards for SUCCESS. If yr skule doesn't believe in them, try to persuade the teachers that they are encouraging things to get and be sure to pat yrself on back when you know you have done something as well as you can. It is V. V. Good for Soul to do so and anything that boosts self-confidence is good for SUCCESS in general.

SCHOOL

SUCCESS at skule can be broken down into the following areas:

1) with frendz

Does anyone in the whole skule **LIKE** me?

2) in sport

3) in some work

2 + 2 = 22 X
3 + 3 = 33 X

4) with teachers

WHO said that?

5) in exams

Arghhhhh!

If you do not feel that you are a winner in any of these areas, pick the one you are most likely to succeed with and concentrate on it till it gets a teeny bit better. Then go on to another. Then go back to the first. Then try a third. Then go back to the second. Don't try for all five cos V. Few Teenage Worriers can manage all of them. But aim, by the time you leave, to feel good about *one* of these areas and possibly two.

SEXISM

As in racism above, sexism is still a force to be reckoned with as boyz look at yr chest rather than yr soul Etck (not the case with *moi*, who has no chest . . .) and when you get out into werld, you can still, if a gurl, hit yr head on glass ceiling when you discover all the best jobz and dosh are still going to blokes. This is improving, but quite slowly, despite wot the newspapers say about babes taking power.

SPIRITUALITY

Adored Father told me once about a play in which a physicist keeps a lucky horseshoe on the door of his laboratory, and then when all his clever mates laugh at him he says he doesn't believe in it really. 'But,' he says, 'they say it goes on working even if you don't believe it.' I don't wish to imply that I think religion is the same as superstition, but it seems to *moi* that the need for the Yuman Race to have religions is V. Closely related to it. The V. Famous psychoanalyst Sigmund Freud (Espesh Famous for thinking SEX was behind everything, and in front of it too, though less so in the case of some of us than others, moan, whinge, examine tape-measure suspiciously Etck) thought Religion was just a symptom of how much we repress all our Dark Thoughts, and when the Yuman Race grew up and learned to live with what goes on in the Inner Recesses of Ye Minde, we'd all just grow out of it.

Also Karl Marx, the Famous German Thinker of V. Clever Thoughts and founder of Marx & Spenders (I made that bit up – L. Chubb) said Religion was the Opium of the People, and was just there to make the Poor and Needy keep their mouths shut and not grumble, because God had decided they should live like that and it was Just Tough – God is therefore V. Convenient for the rich people who hope the poor won't get so fed up about their circs that they try to take their dosh off them Etck.

For *moi*self, I am inclined to think that while a lot of V. Horrible things have certainly been done in the name of various kinds of gods, a lot of V. Horrible things have also been done in the name of Yuman Beings people treated as if they were gods, viz: Hitler Etck. Maybe this means we do have a need to give ourselves up to something beyond the werld inside our own Hedz, and which makes us Feel United With Others, and praps it's better if we accept that and try to do something positive with it, rather than forgetting about it until the next shouting loony shows up with a uniform and a gun. I believe that most SUCCESSful people have some kind of spiritual life, as it is V. Nourishing and can take them away from rigours of workplace Etck.

♥ LOVE BLISS

PEACE TOLERANCE Hope

CALM

SPORT

SUCCESS in ye fields of sport is sought after by nearly all male and lots of female Teenage Worriers, but after you get out of skule it becomes a lot less important, so if you are one of those completely weedy people who can't see ball to hit it Etck, take heart, your failings will not be noticed for the rest of yr life. Nonetheless, sport is V. Good for you, V. Good for character-building stuff like learning to lose gracefully Etck as well as learning to compete (essential part, sadly, of striving for SUCCESS).

CAMPAIGN for more sports fields in tragickly underfunded skules. CAMPAIGN for gurlz football! Get fit and don't be wimpy (wish I could) . . .

Tragick . . . V. Big waste of my only TALENT. Just think If only my Junior SKULE had gone and given gurlz more of a chance . . . gwme moan, whinge . . . .

Example of Moi being V. good sport about wasted football talent Etck. (If I had played, Werld Kup wld be ours . . . Etck Etck).

STARDOM

By now, you shld have an idea that El Chubb is not
interested in being a STAR. I wld hate to be
followed by seedy journalists with vast lenses
watching me pick my hooter and seeing contents of
same Etck. So if stardom is what you want, you may
have wrong buke. Trying to be good at something
may occasionally lead to stardom (ie: Acting) but if
you get it, you are almost bound to regret it. Aim to
earn loads of dosh but keep low profile is El Chubb's
advice. Write to yr favourite star and ask if they
enjoy it. That shld put you off, except they are
bound to lie . . .

TIDINESS

Return of the
lost SOCK

Some Middle-aged Worriers seem to think that
organization is key to SUCCESS, and I have sneaky
feeling that, apart from painters, poets Etck who can
live in hovels happy only with their ART, they may
be right.

I blame my own tragick disorganization on the
fact that my only parents are so V. Lazy and sluttish.
My Adored Father is surrounded by festering piles
of old newspapers that he insists on keeping for his
DIY articles and my mother barely washes a cup by

75

How to TIDY UP
(part 402)

Get THREE boxes or binbags
Label 1, 2, 3.

① Chuck **OUT**
② Give to JUMBLE
③ Keep to **SORT** later

GUIDE TO CATEGORIES

① Bits of fluff, dried up
pens, odd socks, old gum,
bus tickets, small bits
of plastic. Anything
broken.

② Anything NOT broken
you no longer need
or want.

③ Everything else.

Now - all you should have
left is yr bed, cupboard
Etck. There shld be
NOTHING on the
floor (If only it were
so easy. Sigh).

Moi: failing to follow own advice.

waving it under the tap and shaking it, or sometimes running an oil-painty finger over it for especially deep down stains. However, I look at Ashley, whose room, though tiny, gleams like new pin, and realize that it is just that I am a Bad person . . . moan, glume (*Get on with it – Ed*).

Question: Is tidiness genetic? Did Granny Chubb's genes skip my dad and go straight into Ashley, bypassing *moi*? Wld my mother be more tidy Etck if she hadn't had nannies and cleaners running after her picking up each sock and crumb when she was a mere child? Whatever the answer, the tragick consequences of our family history (or herstory as I'm sure all gurlz shld call their lives) is that my Only Mother, having been bought up in conditions like Royal Family Etck, cannot get used to living in slum. Thus, though incapable of doing a hand's turn herself, she is always nagging the rest of us. I am now quite an expert at burning fish fingers and turning sprouts to green liquid just like her . . . We certainly miss Ashley, who used to cook family supper every night, using a proper cookbook (and a couple of saucepans, arf arf) but now he has swanned off to University to save werld, we can only wait and hope that Benjy may have a cooking gene. He tried to cook his hamster once, so there may be a glimmer of hope . . .

Umbrella

Someone once said that a bank is something that will give you an umbrella in fine weather and ask for it back when it rains. SUCCESS is a bit like that. When you are doing well, you tend to do better and better, cos you believe in yrself and so people believe in YOU, and fall over themselves to help you Etck. When you do badly, the whole thing goes into reverse. So, think of that umbrella and always try to have something to fall back on in yr self-esteem buke if one part of your SUCCESS-strategy fails . . . Arg.

Vocals

Yr voice just could be the key to yr SUCCESS, since we live in V. Unfair werld, where high-pitched whine of mosquito is less enchanting to ear than deep buzz of honey bee Etck. Sadly it's sometimes not what you say, but the way that you say it, as Decrepit mangey old class (or clarse) system in Little Britain still rules and oppresses the majority oo carn't speak proper. What El Chubbo has noticed, however, is how the way the Upper clarse people speak has changed over the years. If you look at V. Old Brit movies (as I have been doing in an attempt

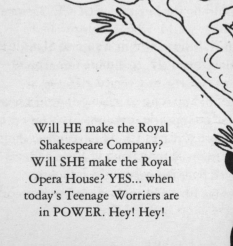

to prepare for my magnificent film career) or even early TV ads, you will notice that even V. Ordinary folk like suburban housewives dusting already immaculate banisters speak with a plum the size of Buckingham Palace in their mouths and a chandelier where their tonsils ought to be. eg: *hice* for 'house', *gawn* for 'gone' Etck. Only the Royal Family speak like that today . . . but it is significant that society is still in thrall to crippling snobbery re lingo. And as it still seems that speaking posh can impress people in Powerful positions, it cld be an idea to brush up your accent until you are powerful and then CAMPAIGN V. V. Haaaard for end to this Snobbery, viz: Only V. Nice, Welsh, Caribbean, and Cockney accents can get power for next five hundred years.

WEDDINGS

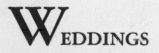

Some Teenage Worriers think it a sign of SUCCESS to get married. (Obviously, it is more of a sign of SUCCESS to ackshully *stay* married.) To *moi*, it seems an odd dream to long to wear daft clothes, to make a bunch of impossible promises in full view of a throng of distant relatives you've never met, snog in front of said grisly throng, sign yr life away, get pissed and go off on holiday being pelted with paper, horseshoes, fake foam Etck. From this you're supposed to Live happily Ever After?

Weddings usually start with engagements, which used to be arranged by parents largely for reasons of property, links with other families Etck, which led to great abuses. Eventually the church made it illegal to arrange the betrothal of children under seven (!) but Arranged Marriages are still quite common in many cultures and as yet I don't know if anyone's done a survey of which kind of marriages are happier . . .

NB El Chubb's tip for a SUCCESSful marriage: you shld just live together for the first twenty years or so and then make an honest man or woman of each other (still wish only parents had tied the knot though, so not sure if this is right. Aargh.)

WISHING-ON-A-STAR

Wells, stars, wishbones, birthday cakes, little blokes calling themselves Rumplestilstkin, strange old bats posing as fairy godmothers – all these play their part in the process called growing up. Pretty soon you realize none of it works, but you go on anyway. And why not? Keeping hope alive is one of the vital keys to SUCCESS in everything you do, dear fellow struggler in the vineyards of Worry, so keep wishing, cos without wishes and hopes you're nowhere.

XCELLENCE

✳ We cannot all be at Peak, Top, dizzying heights Etck. But it can be fun to TRY

OK. I'll admit Xcellence
has its part to play in the
game of SUCCESS but
the famous phrase goes:
✳ 'Lucky? Yeah. The harder
I work, the luckier I get.'
And that's the point:
Xcellence on its own isn't
enough – there's got to be V. Hard work too.
There's no point, frinstance, in having a talent for
drawing unless you draw all the time and improve
it. Excellence is usually 10% talent and 90%
devotion. Even those incredibly few people of real
genius are almost always obsessed by what they do
and do it all the time. El Chubb, being a nachurally
V. Lazy soul, preaches equal amounts of hanging
out, gazing at navel type daydreaming time in order
to pursue crazed luny obsessions . . . For it must be
remembered that even the geniuses are often not
discovered till they are pushing up daisies, so
knowing how to be Happy is more important for a
SUCCESSful life than knowing how to be clever.
Think of poor old Van Gogh, wandering about with
only one ear and never selling a painting. And now
his sunflowers, and even copies of his sunflowers,
sell for small fortune (sob).

Yo-yo

Learn to let go. SUCCESS and failure follow each other as surely as Spring follows Winter. One thing is working, another thing isn't. One door closes, another door closes, blah blah. Most SUCCESSful people truly believe that another door opens, they really do. And for them, it seems to happen. So when you're picked for the skule footie team only to break your leg on the day of the match, or when the results of the Art Competition everyone said you'd win come through and you are not even mentioned in the list of 300 highly recommended entries, DO NOT EVER despair. SUCCESS is not something to take personally. It wafts its wings skittishly, only to swoop elsewhere. Your life is about trying to get it in four main areas: werk, home, people, self. The greatest of these (cos it helps all the others to happen) is self. Not selfishness, but self-esteem. This, sadly, is an item that El Chubb, and most Teenage Worriers, are V. V. Low in. And one knock can send us flying off perch. El Chubb's advice is to read about lives of others. See how V. Complicated, V. Full of highs and lows most lives are and decide that you won't be knocked down by adversity but will struggle up and fight on, so that the yo-yo of life will be buzzing up the string and never dangling at the bottom for too long. To achieve this wondrous state you need . . .

ZEST

Zest is that stuff on outside of orange and lemon peel. Bitter, but zingy. Zest for life is almost universal in SUCCESSful folk: they are doers, triers, smilers, singers, dreamers, thinkers. Having a zest for anything means you are never bored, so even if you live in slum, have no dosh, are abandoned by everyone you care for, if there's one thing you love doing, it can keep your zest for life aflame . . . Find it, nourish it, dearest Teenage Worriers, and the future will be golden path up which you will cheerfully stumble.

FORWARD TO WILD SUCCESS!

Afterword

And now, dearest fellow Teenage Worriers, I reach the end of this humble survey of SUCCESS. I look at my own small life in the vast cosmos of the Yuniverse and I say to myself: Does any of it matter? Does it really matter if I get a single GCSE? Does it matter whether Benjy ever stops worrying about floors? Does it matter if my Adored Father leaves home with another acrobat or my Only Mother hits bottle in despair at fact that she has spent twenty years trying to paint and can still barely hold brush? Does it matter that my own head is a mass of matted phobias, crossed wires and festering worry about V. Small things and V. Large things with no clear line between them? The answer to these questions is, like yr own Life, both . . .

> *Yes*
> *and*
> *No.*

The Yes bit is about SUCCESS. It's about trying to unfurl the bit you can unfurl and using all the positive bits you've got to make everything as good as you possibly can.

The No bit is also about SUCCESS. It's about not caring too much about the things you can't change (so that you can concentrate on the things you can).

And so, my dear reader, turn the page and why not fill in this little summary of yr SUCCESSes now. Put it away for ten years and look at it again then, or even fill it in again? You could do it every ten years, until you are sixty, or seventy, or eighty, or ninety, and see whether a little bit of what you hoped to achieve has happened. And if you get to ninety, you will be SUCCESSful at at least one thing: Living a long life! But what I think will happen is that things that bug you now will have changed in ten or twenty years time, so you can hardly remember WHY they were so important, but that hobbies you cherish now will continue to give you happiness for ever . . .

I end with the following wish: may all yr happy dreams come true and all yr nightmares crumble into dust. And may the rainbow-coloured birdy of SUCCESS lay its egg on your doorstep! (Must put pillow in front of door in case . . .)

Lurve,

×

×

Letty Chubb

Date — and YEAR

Name: Age:

What I wish for MOST in MY life NOW

What I wish for MOST in MY future

What I wish for MOST in the WORLD

What I would MOST like to DO

Things I am PROUD of